UNSTEADY IN LOVE

FAIRLANE SERIES #3

HARLOW LAYNE

Unsteady in Love

A Fairlane Series Novel

HARLOW LAYNE

UNSTEADY IN LOVE by Harlow Layne

ISBN-13: 978-1-950044-02-3 (Ebook Edition)

ISBN-13: 978-1-950044-03-0 (Paperback Edition)

Edited by: Your Editing Lounge - Editor: Kristen

Proofread by: Melita Bloomer & Moonlight Manuscripts

Cover Design: Harlow Layne

Images from Depositphotos.com

PRUE

The Day After High School Graduation

My toes skimmed across the worn wood of the porch as I tried for the hundredth time that day to reach Holden. We were supposed to go to Chicago to try to find ourselves an apartment for the fall, but Holden had failed to pick me up when he was supposed to. At first, I thought nothing of it and only thought he was late, but as time ticked by with no word, I started to get worried. This wasn't like my boyfriend of three years. Holden always called when he was going to be late, which wasn't very often. Hours later and I was a mess, grasping at straws as to where he was and why he wasn't answering any of my phone calls or text messages.

"Any word?" my dad asked out the screen door, worry etched on his strong but tired face.

"No." I hung my head as tears started to build for the millionth time that day.

"Why don't you drive on over to his house? Maybe his parents know where he is. I think leaving the front porch will do you some good anyhow." He gave me a weary smile that did nothing to ease my worries.

"Maybe I should. Sitting here isn't getting me anywhere," I strangled out, worried about what could have happened to Holden to prevent him from picking up his phone.

"That's my girl. I'm sure it's some big misunderstanding." He gave me a wan smile.

"You think?" My head popped up, hopeful.

"Baby girl, Holden loves you more than life itself. Nothing could keep him away."

He did. Holden loved me just as much as I loved him. My dad was right. Long ago, my dad had accepted that Holden would be around for the long haul. Not that Holden was bad news or anything. Only the fact that my dad thought I was too young to find the man I was going to spend the rest of my life with.

This all had to have been some kind of misunderstanding. Holden had probably left his phone somewhere and couldn't hear it the hundred times I'd called. That had to be it.

"You're right, Dad. Thanks. I'm going to see what's going on. Don't wait up for me." I hopped off the porch swing and dashed inside for my car keys. On my way out, I popped up on my toes and gave my dad's smooth cheek a kiss. So excited to see Holden, I tripped going down the stairs. Looking back up at my dad, he stood shaking his head and waved.

The entire way to Holden's house, I had the windows down and let the wind blow through my hair. There was something about the feeling of the night air on my skin and my hair tickling along my back and arms that soothed me. By the time I made it to Holden's house, I almost felt like myself again.

As I pulled up into his driveway, I noticed there were no lights on in the house which was odd. There were always lights on at night from the timer they always set. Stacy and Bruce Montgomery didn't want their son to ever come home to a dark house. This was the first time in years I'd seen it pitch black inside. The worry from earlier reared its ugly head as I hoped a light would miraculously turn on.

Still, I parked and made my way up to the ornate front door. I tried to peek inside through the frosted windows to no avail. I knew there was no point, but I was desperate. It was eerie how quiet the house was. Not even a cricket was chirping in the yard.

Taking a deep breath, I rang the doorbell with the hope that this was all some sort of silly prank and waited patiently for someone to answer the door. After a few minutes with no one in sight, I decided to try my luck at the doorknob. If Holden knew I was coming over, he made sure that the front door was unlocked for me to come in. We'd been together for so long, I was part of the family. This time, though, I was met with the resistance of a locked door.

Where were they?

Fighting back the tears that were threatening to build, I slipped my phone out of my back pocket and punched in Holden's number one last time. By that time, I expected it to ring and go straight to voicemail or for it to be dead after all the times I'd called and texted throughout the day. I never expected the message that shattered my heart into a million pieces.

"We're sorry. You have reached a number that has been disconnected or is no longer in service. If you feel you have reached this recording in error, please check the number and try your call again."

Falling to my knees, my entire world crumbled around me.

Holden was gone.

And I was alone.

1

PRUE

BLURRY EYED, I MADE MY WAY DOWN THE AISLE, choking back the sob that had been threatening to spill out for the past hour. I had three goals in mind that were keeping me focused. Keeping me from making a spectacle of myself. The first was to make my way to my car without speaking to anyone. The second was to drive home without wrecking, and the third was to crawl into bed, pull the blankets up over my head and bawl my eyes out.

With my head down and hands clenched into fists, no one bothered to speak to me. They'd all already said their condolences. What more could they say? It was only a matter of time. I knew it was coming no matter how hard I had tried to deny it.

I was pulled up short when I spotted a large figure leaning against the trunk of my old Ford Taurus. When the figure saw me, he stood up tall. So tall, he was well beyond six foot with a hulking frame that on any other day of the week would have had me quaking in my boots, but not this day. I didn't give one shit who it was or what they wanted. My sole focus was on my goal of making it to my bed to cry. Alone and in peace. That was all I cared about.

Not caring, I ignored the figure, bypassing him and making my way to the driver side door. I could feel him looking at me, his gaze burning a hole in the back of my head, but again, I didn't care. Instead, I hit the button to unlock my door and heard the satisfying sound of my doors unlocking. With my hand on the handle, I felt his heat against my back.

Maybe it wasn't smart for me to throw caution to the wind. In my little town there was very little crime, which gave me a false sense of security, or maybe it was the fact that I had nothing else to live for now that my dad was dead except to pay off his medical bills, which would probably take until the next century.

"Prue, are you really going to ignore me?" a gruff voice asked me. There was something in that voice that rendered my body immobile. It was familiar and yet foreign all at the same time.

Spinning around, I was met with the chocolatey brown eyes of my high school sweetheart. I'd know those eyes anywhere. I'd spent countless hours staring into them before he'd up and left, breaking my heart almost four years ago.

Crossing my arms over my chest to keep my heart from falling out onto the parking lot for him to stomp all over, I narrowed my eyes, peering up at the man who was once familiar but now looked like a total stranger.

Since I'd last seen him, he'd grown at least two inches. In high school, Holden was the captain of the football team, and at the time, I thought he was muscular with his athletic frame. But now those once lean muscles had grown muscles. There were muscles on top of muscles. In essence, Holden was now huge. Almost bodybuilder huge. On top of all those new muscles, his arms were covered in ink. His long-ago baby face was now angular and filled with tension. What was once soft and sweet was now rough and rugged. He was definitely no longer the boy I used to know. He hadn't been for a long time.

"Holden?" My gaze slid down the rest of his body. He was outfitted in tight, dark jeans that looked as if the seams might burst any second from show-casing his magnificent thighs, black motorcycle boots, and a dark gray t-shirt that stretched over his bulging biceps and chest. He was perfection—and I hated him.

"Prue." The one syllable of my name coming from

his lips sounded as if it physically pained him to utter the one syllable.

"What are you doing here?" I eyed the door to the funeral home as people started to trickle out, silently praying they'd keep their distance.

Clearing his throat, he placed his hands in his pockets, making his jeans dip lower on his trim waist. For a brief second, I imagined what he might look like underneath his t-shirt.

Stop noticing his body! This was the man who up and disappeared never be seen again.

"I heard about your dad and wanted to be here for you," he answered with genuine sadness in his voice.

"You wanted to be here for me?" I asked, my words dripping with sarcasm. "Where were you the day after graduation? Where were you when my dad got his diagnosis? Nowhere is where you were. Gone. I didn't need you then, and I sure as hell don't need you now, Holden Montgomery." Fire burned in my veins as the memories of Holden not being by my side when I needed him flickered through my subconscious. My eyes turned to slits as I reached behind me and gripped the door handle to help keep me grounded. "Go back to where you came from."

"Please, Prue. I want to be here for you. I can't…" He faltered, the eyes I once loved filled with sadness. "I can't imagine what you're going through. I know you don't have anyone."

"Do you now? Have you been stalking me?" My anger grew into something I hadn't felt in years. Not since he'd disconnected his phone and left without a trace. All I wanted was to be left alone and go cry in my bed.

"No," his brows knitted together. "You know me, I'd never do that."

"I don't know who you are anymore, and you certainly don't know me. The boy I knew never would have left me without a reason."

Closing his eyes, face etched in agony, Holden nodded. "I'm not that boy anymore. The man standing before you wants to explain what happened after graduation. If only you'll let him."

Hanging my head, I bit back the sob as I whimpered. "Not today, Holden. Please don't do this today. I can't handle it today of all days."

"When?" he demanded, standing even taller. Imposing. If I didn't know better, I would have thought he'd done it to intimidate me.

"I don't know. If you have to do it, then give me time. I'm barely holding it together. If you ever cared for me, you'll let me go."

Hurt flashed across his face for only a moment before he schooled his features. "I'll give you time," he rasped out before turning on his booted heel and walking across the dark parking lot into the night.

I closed my eyes, wanting to yell for him to come back. Maybe he could make the hurt go away even for only a moment. And then I remembered what he'd done to me. He wasn't here to give me comfort. I had no idea what he wanted or why he came back, and I didn't care. Long ago, I had stopped caring about Holden and what he wanted.

2

PRUE

MY EYES BLINKED OPEN AS THE DOORBELL RANG FOR the third time in thirty seconds. I could barely open my eyes from all the crying I'd done once I got home last night.

The doorbell rang again. And again.

Whoever it was, wasn't giving up.

Clearing my eyes, I looked at my alarm clock to see it was a little after seven in the morning. Who the hell would be ringing my doorbell so early? It better not be someone with a damn casserole. The only person who ever came over was my neighbor, Alex. Shit, was it her? I did notice she was back in town the other day. Maybe it was an emergency.

Jumping out of bed, I quickly made my way to the front door not even bothering to check to see who was there.

Big mistake.

Swinging the door open, Holden was taking up the entire door frame with his big body. His legs spread wide and hands clasped onto the top of the door frame.

"What are you doing here, Holden?" I snapped.

"I came to talk. To explain myself."

Wrapping my arms around myself to keep the chill of the cold morning air away, I glared up at him. "Did you ever think that maybe I just might be sleeping?"

"I wanted to catch up before you took off or something, so you wouldn't have to see me," he stated, his voice void of any emotion.

"Are you shitting me? You've got me confused with yourself," I snarled out.

Crossing his own arms over his broad chest, Holden held his ground with his face set, letting me know with one stubborn look he wasn't going to give up until I listened to what he had to say. I hated that damn look, and seeing it after all these years, I wanted to slap it off his stupid, handsome face.

"Listen, I just want to sleep and grieve. Is that too much to ask? Come by next week and we can talk then, if you insist." Hopefully, he'd be over his need to explain why he disappeared almost four years ago.

Shaking his head, his mouth formed into a thin line. "No can do. I'll be gone by then."

"Oh, planning on leaving again, are you? Then don't bother. Maybe I'll see you in another four years."

"Goddammit, Prue, if you'd only listen," he growled out.

"I don't have to listen to anything you have to say. Please just leave me alone," I croaked out.

"Not until you listen to me."

Rage like I'd never felt before consumed me. Why couldn't he leave me alone? It was too much to deal with right now. Or maybe ever, if I was honest with myself.

"Get the hell off my property, Holden! You are not welcome here!" I shrieked, my whole body trembling.

"Why do you always have to be so damn stubborn? Just listen to me for two minutes. That's all, and you never have to see me again if you don't want to." A growl ripped from his chest. His voice was so low and scary, I took a step back.

"You have no right to be here! I don't want to talk to you or see you ever again! Leave like you did before, Holden. Leave!"

Crossing the yard, a tall blond man who looked like a Viking god, dressed in only a pair of pajama pants and tennis shoes, made his way toward us.

"You need to leave," the man said with a slight accent as he came to stand in front of me. "The lady doesn't want you here. If you don't back off, I'll be forced to call the police."

Taking a step back, Holden glared at our guest. "This isn't any of your business. I only want to talk to her."

"She doesn't look like she wants to talk. In fact, she looked scared when I walked up here," the Viking said, standing tall. Protecting me. Who was this man?

Deep lines raced across Holden's forehead, his lips turning down. "Prue," he shook his head, sorrow filling his once familiar eyes, "I would never hurt you."

"I know," I whispered. My vision blurred as tears welled in my eyes. "Please go, Holden. I can't do this."

A flash of emotion crossed his face before Holden turned around and stalked off to a car at the curb. And just like last night and all those years before, he was gone. I had a feeling it wouldn't be the last time I saw Holden Montgomery no matter how much I didn't want to see him again.

The Viking turned toward me with his lips tipped up in a friendly smile making him all the more good looking. "Are you okay?"

Taking a deep breath, I nodded. "Yeah, well, not really." My brows pulled together thinking about where he'd come from. "I don't mean to be rude, but who are you?"

"Oh, I'm sorry," he held his hand out for me to

shake. "I'm Luke Sandström. I'm Alex's boyfriend. The yelling woke up Mason, and I came over to make sure everything was okay."

"Shit." I glanced over at Alex's house. "I'm sorry I woke you up. I'm Prue, it's nice to meet you." I extended my hand and shook his surprisingly warm one. "Please come in for a moment and get out of the cold."

Luke waved his hand in dismissal but followed me inside.

Closing the door, I tried my best to smile up at Luke, but I knew it looked forced. "Thank you for coming over and making sure I was okay. Alex must be happy you're here."

"We both are. We don't get to spend much time together," he answered, eyes dreamy at the notion of his girlfriend.

Seeing how much he loved Alex made me want to cry. I missed that feeling. I missed being in the arms of a man and having someone to talk to.

"Hey, are you okay?" Luke asked with concern etched on his face.

"It's been a hard few days," I answered back softly. *Or months. Or years.*

"I'm sorry," he said sincerely. "If you're okay, I'll leave you be. Is there anything you need?"

"No, but thank you."

Walking Luke to the door, he stopped and stared at something on the table by the door for a moment before turning back to me. "If you need anything, we're right next door. Don't hesitate to ask."

"Thanks." I tried to give him a reassuring smile. "Again, it was nice meeting you."

"You too."

Heading back to my bedroom, I buried my head in my pillow and screamed. Why did Holden have to show up at one of the worst times in my life?

I screamed and cried at the gaping hole that had been left in my heart now that my dad was gone and from seeing Holden again.

My doorbell rang for the second time that day and I swore to myself that if it was Holden, I would call the police on him. Had he waited until Luke was gone to come back?

Opening the door, I was surprised to see Alex standing there. She was beautiful as always, but today she had a glow about her. One that I was sure Luke had put there. When our eyes locked, I saw the tears she was holding back.

Staying silent, I headed back to my bedroom. It was the only room I could be in without seeing my dad's ghost. Crawling up on the bed, I curled into a ball.

"Prue, sweetie. Are you okay? Is there anything I

can do for you? Luke told me about your dad," she said barely above a whisper, rubbing my back.

"Can you bring him back, cancer free?" I asked brokenly.

"I wish I could." Picking up my hand, she held it as I cried silently. "I'm so sorry, Prue. He was such a great man, and I'm going to miss him. Can I make you a cup of tea or anything?"

"No, I don't want anything but to be left to mourn my father in peace."

"Who was that guy who was here earlier? Do we need to be worried about him?" she asked curiously.

Turning into my pillow, I cried out. Alex rubbed up and down my back, trying her best to soothe me. Little did she know there was nothing that could have made the hurt go away. I'd been trying for the past three and a half years.

"What is it, sweetie?"

"It's Holden," I sobbed. The memories of our time together flashed before me until they were finished. Gone. Just like he was gone that day. "He's back for some reason and showed up here demanding to speak to me. Saying he was already here and heard about my dad."

"Who is he to you?"

"The man who broke my heart," I cried out. "I

don't want to talk about him though. I don't want to remember what he did to me."

"Do I need to be worried that he'll come back?"

Turning toward her, I promised, "He's not violent if that's what you're thinking."

"I wasn't sure what to think." Wrapping me in her arms, she let me cry on her shoulder until there were no more tears left to cry.

"Um…I hate to bring this up now," she looked at me sheepishly. "I haven't had a chance to talk to you since I got back from Mexico, but I'm moving."

"What? Really? Where? When?" I giggled, and it made her smile. "Oh, gosh, listen to me and all my questions."

It felt freeing to laugh. I couldn't remember the last time I'd even broken a smile let alone laughed.

"Don't worry about it. I'd have the same questions if it were you who was moving. I'm moving tomorrow, but it's still in town, so we can see each other whenever. The deal was too amazing to pass up, and eventually, Luke will move in too."

I sat up against my headboard with wide eyes. I knew she liked Luke. A lot. But I had no idea it was to the point of them moving in together. "Wow. Things are really serious between the two of you. I guess Mexico was a hit."

A smile spread across her tanned face. "It was

amazing, and so is Luke. Every day, I wake up and have to pinch myself to make sure I'm not dreaming. How am I living this life? How did I get so lucky to have such an incredible man find me and get along with Mason so well? It's wonderful and sad at the same time to see. Mason's father has never given him the time of day, and Luke listens to every single word he has to say. Right now, they're making pancakes together." Happy tears filled both our eyes.

"Oh, Alex, I'm so happy for you. And Mason." Leaping forward, I wrapped my arms around her in a hug. No one deserved a happy life more than Alex. On more than one occasion, I had witnessed her ex standing outside her house yelling and swearing at her. Threatening her.

"Thank you. I didn't mean to make this about me, but I didn't want you to find out I was moving when you saw the truck show up in the morning. We won't be far, and you can come over anytime or call if you need me. Please, it's going to be so weird at first being in a new house. I need someone to help me pick out furniture because I can't decorate to save my life."

"I'd be happy to help. Just tell me when you need me. It'll help keep my mind off of my dad and Holden."

"If you need a place to get away or hide from Holden, just say the word. I'd be happy to help. If you're sure you don't need anything, I should probably get home to help pack. I have no clue how he packs, and I'd like to know where all my stuff is since he'll be leaving me to do all the unpacking, and I won't be able to ask him where everything is every time I can't find something."

"Thank you for coming by to make sure I was okay. I really appreciate it. I'm going to miss you and our talks, even as infrequent as they were."

"Call me if you need anything. I mean it. Day or night, I'm here for you, and I'll miss you, too."

"I will, I promise."

We hugged once more before she left.

This time as I headed back to bed, I felt a little bit lighter.

I wasn't as alone as I thought I was.

I had Alex. Even if she was moving away.

3

HOLDEN

I held my breath as I waited for Prue to answer her door. I'd given her two days, and I would have given her more if I could, but I was shipping out in a matter of days. Time was running out for me to explain to her why I'd disappeared after graduation.

The front door swung open to a scowling Prue standing with her hands on her hips. "Look who came at a decent time."

"For that, I really am sorry. I truly thought that you might disappear so you wouldn't have to deal with me." I tried to explain.

Never in all the years when I thought I'd see Prue again did I think it would be immediately after her father's funeral. I knew she would be pissed at me, and I didn't blame her, but now I wasn't sure if she'd ever listen to me.

"Like I said before, I'm not the one who runs," she bit out.

I didn't remember her being so feisty.

"Can I come in? It's cold as hell out here."

Letting out an annoyed breath, she stepped back from the door, and I got my first look into her house. It was small. Smaller than the house she'd grown up in. I saw the couch that we had spent many hours making out on now more worn out. The table I'd sat at and eaten more than my fair share of dinners at had a few extra scuffs on it. Almost everything was the same as it once was just in a different place and more worn.

The one thing that had drastically changed was Prue. She was more beautiful now than she had been back in high school. She was stunning and all woman. Her curves had filled out even though she was skinnier than ever. Her hair was long, down past the middle of her back, and her eyes held more hurt in them than she ever deserved.

I knew I'd put some of that hurt there, and I was ready to try to ease her pain.

"I was about to make a cup of coffee. Do you want some?"

"No, thanks. You never used to drink coffee." I blurted out the last part, but once it was out, I wished I hadn't.

Tilting her head, her gaze turned cold. "I never used to do a lot of things I do now."

Shit. I had my work cut out for me. Not that I thought otherwise when I had decided to find her, but I thought she might hear me out. Now, not so much.

I followed her as she headed into the kitchen but stopped at the dining room table when she turned to look at me over her shoulder with a withering look. Fine, she needed her space. I could give her that for a couple more minutes.

There were papers scattered all over the table. With the surface covered, it didn't look as if it had been used to eat at in a long time. I didn't mean to be nosy, but when I spotted more than one 'past due' and 'final notice' in red, I couldn't help but look. They weren't just papers, but bills, and all of them were preparing to cut services or send her debt to collections.

What the hell?

"You didn't used to be a snoop," Prue brushed passed me, making her way to the living room.

"Well, it seemed like you didn't want me to follow you into the kitchen, and then…I saw all the red."

"Which is none of your business. Say what you came to say, Holden," she said with clear annoyance in her cool tone while sitting down in the recliner.

Taking a seat on the couch, I turned toward her, ready to try to explain.

"Please hear me out before you speak. At the time, I thought what I did was the best decision I could make."

"So, you don't believe that now?"

"What did I ask?" I said, trying to keep my cool.

Her eyes went round, and her voice filled with sarcasm. "Excuse me. Go ahead."

"To answer your question, no I don't know if it was for the best. I was young and in shock. I didn't know what to do." Running my hand through my cropped hair, I steeled myself for what I was about to tell her and the tears that I was likely to see. "After graduation and we split up for the night, I went to dinner with my parents. It was surreal. Earlier that day, they were acting strange, but I thought nothing of it. Just that they were sad their only child was graduating high school and would soon be moving out and headed to college." Taking a deep breath, I rubbed my sweaty hands on my jeans. "Do you remember when my grandfather died?"

"Yeah, I remember, but what does that have to do with what happened after graduation?"

"Well, my parents failed to mention at the time of his death that he left me a sizable fortune under the condition that I marry before I turn twenty-five."

This was where it got messy.

I could tell she wanted to say something, but she

kept to her word and stayed silent. Except for her tapping her fingernails on her coffee cup.

"I thought no problem. Right? Because I planned to marry you after we graduated, but my parents had a different idea." Shock and hurt flashed in her eyes, but I continued on, needing to get my story out. "They had the rest of my life planned out for me, and none of it included what I wanted. They already had someone picked out who I was supposed to marry. They even wanted me to change my degree. No longer was I going to be an architect, but a lawyer, following in my family's footsteps."

I had always hated seeing Prue cry, and now was no different. My heart broke as I watched tears well up ready to spill over. Shaking my head, I leaned forward, putting my elbows to my knees. "They refused to pay my tuition if I didn't do exactly what they planned. I didn't care until they threatened to call Loyola and get your scholarship revoked."

"What?" Prue cried out in a whisper.

"I didn't believe them. Why would I? They loved you. Not once had they ever given me a reason to think otherwise. It wasn't until my dad took out his phone and called the dean to your college that I knew they were serious. I couldn't let them take away your scholarship or fuck up your life like they were trying to fuck up mine."

"Are you married, Holden?" she choked out. Her eyes held more pain in that moment than they had after seeing her outside the funeral home. There was no way in hell I would ever marry anyone but her.

"Fuck, no! I wasn't going to let them win," I growled out. "They thought if they threatened your schooling, I'd do what they wanted. I did the opposite of what they wanted. I enlisted in the Marines. I wasn't going to let them ruin both our lives."

"Didn't you think I should have had a say in the matter?" she croaked out.

"Now, I do, but at the time, I only wanted to make sure you could go to school to be a nurse. I knew how important it was to you."

"You were more important to me than becoming a nurse," she whimpered. "I can't believe you did that to us, Holden."

"I know," I hung my head. There wasn't a day that had gone by when I hadn't questioned my decision to enlist. "I'm sorry, Prue. I really am. I tried to get ahold of you once bootcamp was over, but you were already gone. It wasn't until a couple of months ago that I found out where you were, and I had to wait until I was on leave to see you."

Locking my eyes with hers, I reached out to clasp her hand. For a moment, she tensed but then relaxed under my touch. "I have to go back in a few days, and I couldn't imagine waiting another six months to talk to you. I know this is the worst timing with your dad dying. Again, I'm so sorry, and I hope that one day you'll be able to forgive me."

Tears freely trekked down her cheeks with abandon, breaking my heart. Her green eyes held so much sadness in them, they seemed endless.

"I hope one day I'll be able to forgive you too," she said so softly I barely heard her.

"Is there anything I can do for you?" *Like pay the giant stack of bills sitting on your table.*

"Can you turn back time?"

"If I could, I would," I replied honestly.

I knew that she meant to bring her dad back, but I couldn't help but think deep down she meant about after our high school graduation too.

Abruptly, Prue stood and wiped her tears away with the tips of her fingertips. "Well, thank you for coming back and explaining. I've got a lot to do. I need to try to get my job back, and I have very little time to do it in."

"What happened with your job?"

Was that why her bills were left unpaid?

"Oh," she looked away. "I asked to take leave to take care of my dad. I needed my job for the health insurance, but it didn't cover the expense of someone looking after him. I couldn't have both. Instead, after a week of me taking leave, they fired me. No one else would hire me with the hours I needed."

"Fuck, Prue, I'm sorry."

"Not your fault, but I really need to figure things out before…" She bit her bottom lip and it took everything within me to not to pull it loose and crush my lips to hers.

Standing, I headed to the front door. "I'd like to see you again before I have to leave. Would that be okay?"

"I don't know, Holden. While it was nice to finally know why you up and disappeared, it's still hard to be around you. Too many memories." She peered up at me from beneath her wet lashes, and all I wanted to do in that moment was hold her in my arms.

Her heart wasn't the only one that broke when I left. I wanted to mend both our broken hearts and start living the life we had planned all those years ago.

"Don't you pull those sad, puppy dog eyes on me, Holden Montgomery. You know I could never deny you when you pulled those out."

Was I? Well, if it worked so I could see her again, I wasn't going to stop.

"Fine," she huffed, tapping her foot. "I have a few job interviews tomorrow, so why don't you come by sometime in the late afternoon?"

"Or I could take you to dinner," I offered, knowing I was pushing my luck.

She looked as if she could use a good meal or a hundred. Did she not have the money to buy the food she needed or was it from taking care of her dad and not herself?

"I don't know, Holden."

This time, I intentionally pulled out the puppy dog eyes and even stuck my lower lip out a little.

"Fine, but don't think you can keep pulling that shit, and I'll fall for it. Just to let you know, the pouting lip thing doesn't work anymore. You're too…" she tilted her head in a way that meant she's trying to find a nice way to say what she was about to say.

"What?" I laughed.

"You're too manly," she shrugged. "Too rugged to pull it off."

"Whatever you say, Prue," I chuckled. This had turned out better than I thought it would. "I'll see you tomorrow night. I'll pick you up at seven."

"Uh, yeah, sure." She nodded awkwardly.

I could tell she didn't want to meet again, but I wasn't going to give up until I got what I had come for.

And that was Prue.

The love of my life and the one who had kept me going after all these years apart.

4

How had I gotten myself into this mess? I didn't want to see Holden again, let alone have dinner with him. But those damn puppy dog eyes did me in. Whenever he had wanted to get his way and I had disagreed, which hadn't been often, Holden had always known how to get me to cave.

I didn't know what he thought we had to talk about. I'd listened to what he had to say, and I did understand that he'd thought he was doing what was best for us, but it still didn't make it hurt any less after all these years. I'd thought of his mom and dad as family and it broke my heart all over again to learn they had wanted Holden to marry someone else and that they'd probably been planning it since his grandfather died.

I paced from the living room into the kitchen and back, and each time I couldn't help but look over and see all the bills that were piled up on the table. My interviews had gone well, but no one was hiring in my small town, and I wasn't sure if I could afford to commute to Riverside or any of the other surrounding cities. It didn't matter if I could afford it because if I didn't get a job and soon, I was going to be homeless. Tomorrow I would look into expanding my search, and I wouldn't stop until I was employed.

The sharp knock on the door broke me out of my musings. Taking in a deep breath, I tried to clear my mind of being out of a job and all the money I now owed. No longer would I have my dad's disability check to help pay for all the medical bills.

Opening the door, I was shocked to see Holden in a black button-down shirt and dark jeans. He looked nice. Beyond nice, but I didn't want to think about how hot he was and the man he'd become.

"Are you ready?" he asked a little gruffly.

"Yeah, let me get my purse and lock up. Where are we going?"

"Wherever you suggest."

"Oh, well, I don't know. I can't remember the last time I went out to dinner. Hmmm…" It had been so long since I'd had extra money for such an expense. Not that I had any now, but I couldn't say no to those damn eyes. "My neighbor Alex, you met her boyfriend the other day—"

"Good neighbors to have. Looking out for you." He nodded, ushering me down the steps to his car.

"Actually, she moved." And it sucked. Alex was my only friend, and now that we weren't neighbors anymore, I wasn't sure when I'd see her. "Anyhow, she loves this Italian restaurant, so we could go there. She always raved about it and tried to get me to go with her a couple of times."

"Give me directions. I've been here a couple of days, but I still don't know my way around." His brows pinched together. "Did your neighbor move far away?"

Putting my seatbelt on, I gave him directions. My town was small, so we had to go to a nearby town to eat, but it wasn't far. "I'm not really sure where she moved to, but Fairlane isn't too big, so she can't be that far. But she isn't next door anymore."

Sitting so close to him was distracting. He smelled like home. The aroma of spice and warmth. But then I remembered; he wasn't home. Holden was nothing to me and never would be again.

"Turn here?" I confirmed it was the right turn. "Is she a good friend?" he asked, looking over at me.

"My only friend really, but yeah she's a good friend. Her little boy is so cute and sweet." I smiled thinking of Mason's adorable face. "I'm glad she's got Luke now, and with her no longer being my neighbor, that means no more of hearing her ex-husband yelling outside her house."

Holden grunted beside me. I had no idea what it meant, and I didn't really care. I hated how easy it was for me to talk to him. There was no point in opening up to him. I needed to remember how he had left me and was leaving again in a matter of days. We were quiet for the rest of the short ride to the restaurant. I was excited to try the food that Alex had been raving about since it opened.

Once seated, there was an awkwardness in the air. Neither one of us knew what to talk about. I didn't want to talk about the past. To bring up the old hurt. And I had nothing to speak about for the future either. Luckily, a waitress brought fresh bread and butter to the table and asked what we wanted to drink. I didn't miss the way her eyes hooded as she took Holden in. He didn't even spare her a glance as he ordered a water and continued to peruse the menu.

"Did you know there's only one hotel in your town?" Holden asked as he set his menu down and buttered up his bread.

"Most people stay a couple of towns over in River-side. We don't get many tourists here."

"Why'd you move here?" His eyes gleamed with curiosity from across the table.

Did I want to tell him the truth? No, I didn't, but I knew he would be able to tell if I was lying.

Picking up my menu to hide behind, I read over their amazing selections. It was almost impossible to pick only one thing to eat. Everything sounded good, making my stomach rumble. It had been too long since I'd had a decent meal. Taking a deep breath, I let it out slowly and peeked over the menu to find Holden watching me.

"It was too hard to stay in Oak Park. Everything reminded me of you, and when all I did was cry, my dad suggested we move. I applied to schools in Missouri, and after I was accepted to one in Riverside, we relocated to Fairlane."

I continued to look over the menu to avoid looking at Holden. It wasn't until his hand covered mine that I dropped the menu and pulled my hand back, cradling it to my chest as if he'd wounded me with just his touch.

But hadn't he?

"I'm sorry, Prue." He closed his eyes, and I could see the pain strain his rugged face.

"After graduation, my life changed in so many ways." I shook my head at everything I'd gone through. "You broke me. Shattered my heart into a million and one pieces to never be put back together again. And then," I closed my eyes as my chin trembled, "a week later we found out that my dad had lung cancer. Can you believe that? Never smoked a day in his life, and he got fucking lung cancer."

"He didn't deserve to get cancer." Holden's eyes turned sad. "If I could turn back time, I would have never left. I would have been there for you and your dad and helped you."

"But you did leave, Holden. You left, only to show up at my father's funeral. I needed you and you were gone." I couldn't keep the hurt from my tone.

"I—"

The waitress, who only had eyes for him, interrupted him. I wasn't sure if she even knew I was there until Holden motioned to me. His deep brown eyes filled with sorrow. He cleared his throat and nodded toward me. "Prue, you first."

I'd barely completed my order when the waitress pressed her ample chest up against his arm. What the hell?

"I'm going to go use the restroom and give you two a moment." I was unsure if I hid the jealousy that was running rampant through my veins, but in that moment I didn't care. I needed to get away.

Briskly walking to the bathroom, I threw open the door and leaned against the sink. I had to remind myself that I didn't care if women threw themselves at

Holden or if he was interested in them. That ship had sailed a long time ago.

Splashing some cool water on my face made me feel slightly better and helped clear my mind of stupid thoughts about Holden. Still, I walked back to our table slowly, in no rush to have to sit across from the man I'd once loved or to see the waitress blatantly flirting with him.

"Are you okay?" he asked the moment I sat down across from him in our booth.

"Fine. Why do you ask?" I feigned ignorance of what he could possibly be talking about.

"You were gone…never mind. How'd the job interviews go today?"

"Ugh," I blew out a frustrated breath. "The interviews were fine, but none of them are hiring. They said they'd put me on their list and call if there was an opening. I guess I'm going to have to expand my search to other towns around the area."

"And you don't want to do that?" His brows furrowed in confusion.

I didn't want to explain to him why I didn't want to get a job elsewhere.

"And don't lie to me either," he narrowed his eyes at me.

"Fine," I huffed. "I can't afford the gas to commute. I'll probably have to sell the house to pay off some of the medical bills, so I guess it doesn't matter where I find a job since I'll have to move anyway."

There was a part of me that wanted to move to get away from the memories of my dad. In every room, there were memories that felt as if I might buckle underneath the pain of missing him. But I was afraid if I left, I'd eventually forget him.

"Here you go." The waitress set our food down in front of us. I swear she had undone a couple of buttons on her shirt to show off more cleavage. "If you need *anything* else don't be shy to ask."

I didn't care how good the food was, I didn't think I'd ever be coming back. I rolled my eyes and dipped one of the fried zucchini sticks into the marinara before taking a bite.

"Mmmm," I groaned. It was amazing. The sauce was just the right amount of sweet and tangy and the zucchini was crispy. I wanted to gobble them all down before Holden could get his hands on them.

"Good?" he asked on a chuckle.

"So good. I was thinking I'd never come back, but damn I don't think I could ever give these up. I don't know how Alex brings Luke here. Maybe he goes incognito or something because I can't imagine her enjoying herself if the waitresses all throw themselves at him."

His brows knit. "Did you not want to come back

because of the flirty waitress?"

"Flirting is an understatement. She acted like it's her job to throw herself at good looking men." I shook my head in disgust until I took another bite of zucchini goodness.

"Why would your neighbor's boyfriend need to come incognito?" he asked before he took a bite of the fried zucchini. "Damn, this is good." He dunked his piece in the sauce again.

"I know, right! Don't eat any more of them because I want them all for myself." I laughed before pulling the plate closer to me and taking another bite.

"How about I get us another order?"

Oh, I was sure the waitress would love to come back and all but sit in his lap. Instead of saying that, I deflected. "If you want more, you probably should."

"I definitely want more," he said with so much conviction in his voice I was sure he couldn't be talking about the food anymore.

Taking another bite, I chewed and chewed and chewed. I hated that I was jealous and still attracted to Holden. I needed to get a handle on my feelings. I didn't want to get hurt again when he left in a few days.

"So, your neighbor's boyfriend?" he prompted.

"Luke, right. He's on some super popular show on H@T and has done a few movies. We haven't had cable in forever, and I can't remember the last time I went to see a movie, so I didn't know who he was until he introduced himself. I should have had Alex show me a picture. Not only is he famous, but he's hot as hell. I don't know how she handles all the women who throw themselves at him. Especially with the long distance."

"He doesn't live here?"

"Not right now. He lives in LA where he shoots his show, but I guess he'll be moving here this summer."

"It's pretty cool that you know a movie star," he grumbled. It was obvious he didn't think it was cool at all.

"I don't really know him. The other day was the first time I met him. I only know what Alex has told me, but she is head over heels in love with him." I sighed wistfully. One day, I wanted what Alex and Luke had. I didn't want to be alone forever.

Taking a bite out of my chicken parmigiana, I closed my eyes. Damn, this place made good food. Now I knew why Alex came as often as she did. I could eat this every day.

"I want you to marry me," Holden blurted out of nowhere.

5

WAIT! WHAT?

I coughed and choked on my food almost spitting it across the table. "What?" I gasped out. Surely, I'd heard him wrong.

"I want you to marry me."

"Are you out of your mind?" I sputtered. "Did you get hit by something radioactive while you've been gone?"

"No," he laughed. "Just hear me out. I think I have a solution to both our problems."

Oh, how romantic.

"Don't give me that look. Listen, I saw the bills yesterday. I know you're drowning in debt, and I also know that I'm not your favorite person right now, but if we got married, then I could get my inheritance and pay off all your debt. I'll let you buy any house of your choosing, and then when we get divorced, you can have the house." He shrugged.

He fucking shrugged. Hey, let's get married and divorced. How lovely.

"Divorced?" I asked with a curl of my upper lip.

"Stay married to me for two years. When I get out of the military and come home, you can file for divorce. You get the house, and I don't know…" He shrugged. Again. "A million dollars for your trouble."

How much money was he getting from this inheritance of his?

"That's a lot, Holden. If you want your money, surely you can find someone who will marry you and agree to those terms. You don't need me."

"But I want you. I want to help you. I need to help you after what I put you through. You deserve it."

The sincerity that radiated off him blew my mind away. Holden was serious. He wanted to marry me, pay off my debt, buy me a house, and give me a million dollars. And in two years get divorced.

"You won't have to work if you don't want to. I'll pay all the bills. What more can you ask for?"

I want the first time a man asks me to marry him to be for love and not money. To be married for love and not convenience.

"Holden," I choked out his name trying my best not to cry. "How many times do you plan on getting married? You should marry for love, not to get your money."

Holden's face turned to stone, but he couldn't hide the emotion that played out in his eyes. Before I could try to read what he could possibly be feeling, Holden leaned back, and his face fell back into shadow.

"Let me do this for you. I'll be out of your hair in a couple of days and won't be back for almost a year."

"You would want to do this before you leave?" I shrieked and then clamped my mouth closed when everyone in the restaurant turned to look at me. "Sorry. Carry on," I dismissed them, blushing.

"If we wait until I get back, it wouldn't help you," he said as calmly as if he were discussing the weather.

"What about your parents? Can't they contest your inheritance if you marry me?" I stuttered out, grasping at straws.

"I haven't spoken to my family since I left after graduation. I'll admit if I had talked to a lawyer back then about what they were threatening about my inheritance, I would have found out everything they said was invalid. They knew it, but they were trying to scare me." He leaned forward, putting his elbows on the table. "The one thing they weren't lying about was getting your scholarship revoked. They would have done it. I have no doubt. I only wish I knew then what I know now. All of this could have been avoided."

"I don't know what to say," I rasped out.

"Say yes," his eyes begged.

"I'd ask for time to think about it, but you don't have time."

"We can go to the courthouse tomorrow," he stated as if he had it all planned out. "Prue, I want to make up for leaving you. Let me do this. I'm hoping with time, you'll forgive me, and we can be friends."

I pointed at him, and if he'd been standing in front of me, I would have poked him in the chest. Hard. "You're lucky I'm even talking to you."

"I know, Prue. I know. Don't think that's gone unnoticed. You're probably in shock, but I'm going to take advantage." He frowned. "I want to help you. When I get my inheritance, what I'm offering will be a drop in the bucket. We can sign the papers after we're married and within a month, all your bills will be paid off, and you could be in a new house."

"This feels wrong," I said on a sigh.

"Because you hate asking for help, and you feel like it's charity. Trust me, it's nothing like that. Think of it as helping me get my inheritance and the benefits you'll get for helping me."

Shaking my head, a faint smile ghosted across my face. "You have plenty of time to find someone to marry you once you get back. To find love. You don't need me."

"I do need you because I know and trust you." There was something in his look that told me there was more to it, but he wouldn't tell me no matter how hard I tried. "I'll give you until morning to think about it. I'll pick you up around ten."

"I haven't agreed."

"Yet. You haven't agreed yet."

6

HOLDEN

Prue fidgeted in her seat as I drove us to the courthouse. We hadn't spoken when I picked her up. Instead, she'd been waiting by the door, ready to bolt out of the house when I showed up. I knew she had something to say but hadn't worked up the nerve yet.

Was she going to back out?

"Don't you think I should sign a prenup?" she croaked out, her throat raw.

Stunned, I briefly looked over at her. "I trust you."

"You don't know me anymore. The Prue you once knew is gone." She rested her forehead against the window, staring out. "That should be obvious because the old Prue never would have done this." Her voice was barely more than a whisper, but I could hear the hurt and sadness.

My heart lurched in my chest hearing the sadness

in her voice. She didn't want to marry me. Hell, she didn't even want to be in the car with me. But I needed her tied to me, otherwise Prue would drop out of my life once I was deployed and I'd likely never see or hear from her again.

"I don't think you're that different. Neither of us are deep down where it matters."

"You certainly look different. I hardly recognized you when you came up to me in the parking lot," she muttered.

My appearance *had* changed, but fundamentally I was the same, or so I thought.

A grin tugged at my lips. "I could spot you from a mile away. You're more beautiful now, but that doesn't surprise me. You know the saying, everything gets better with age."

"Oh, please, Holden. You don't need to butter me up. I'm here aren't I?" she gritted out.

For some reason, growing up poor had warped the way Prue saw herself. From the time we met, she could never accept a compliment and never believed me whenever I told her she was beautiful. Just like now. Her gorgeous, light-green eyes stared at me with emotion swimming in them. If she knew that I was marrying her because I loved her and didn't plan to let her go, she never would have agreed.

"Don't you have anything white or cream to wear? You look…"

Like you're going to a funeral.

"I thought it was befitting the mood. Besides, it's not like I'm a virgin. You saw to that," she snorted.

Had Prue had other boyfriends since I'd left? I couldn't handle the thought of her with other men. Just the thought made me see red.

I had made us wait until she was eighteen before we had sex. At the time, I thought we had the rest of our lives together, and Prue hadn't wanted to wait.

Why did I fuck everything up? Everything I thought I'd done for the right reasons had blown up in my face. Could I have had Prue this entire time? Would she ever forgive me?

"When I used to picture our wedding day, it never looked like this." Her face fell, and tears filled her eyes.

I desperately wanted to tell her that we could have another wedding someday. The one she dreamed of. She could have everything if only she stayed with me. "I'm sorry, Prue. You'll never know how sorry I am," I choked out.

"Are you sure you want to do this? Because you'll have plenty of time to find someone after you get back." She rubbed her hands down her pants and picked at some imaginary lint.

"I'm sure."

My hands gripped the steering wheel until my

knuckles turned white, sure that at any moment Prue would ask me to turn the car around and take her back to her house. Once again, we fell silent and didn't speak another word until we stood outside the judge's door.

Looking down to meet her gaze, I placed my palm on the small of her back. "You ready for this?" I asked anxiously. My heart skipped a beat waiting for her answer.

She bit her lip and looked down at her shoes, then without a word, she pushed open the door and stepped inside. Prue twisted her fingers together as I spoke with the sweet old lady who took our marriage certificate and ushered us into the judge's office.

"I don't get a lot of couples coming in to get married anymore," Judge Street said with a kind smile. "May I ask why you chose this route to get married?"

Prue's eyes widened, unprepared to answer any questions. I only hoped she wouldn't correct me.

"Well, sir," I clasped my hands behind my back. "I'm going to be deployed back to the Middle East in a couple of days, and we wanted to get married before I leave."

"And how long have you been together?" he asked with a raised brow.

"Since high school, sir," I answered, hoping he couldn't tell I was lying.

Prue chewed on the inside of her cheek looking anywhere but at us.

"Well, I appreciate your service and would be happy to marry the two of you. All you have to do is stand right there facing each other. Now, hold hands and repeat after me."

I was sure I repeated the appropriate words when they were supposed to be spoken, but my sole focus was on Prue and the emotion that built in her eyes with each spoken word. Tears threatened to spill down her ivory cheeks as I held her shaking hands in mine.

"Holden and Prue, by the power invested in me, I now pronounce you husband and wife. You may now kiss the bride."

Leaning down slowly, I tried to express with my eyes we needed this to look real and for Prue not to freak out when I kissed her. The moment our lips touched for the first time in almost four years, my body flushed with heat and need. Prue stiffened under my touch for only a moment before her body melted into mine and kissed me back. As quickly as she thawed, Prue placed her hands on my chest and pushed me away. With pink cheeks she looked down at her wedding ring, eyes burning with emotion.

My thumb rubbed against the cool steel that now rested on my left hand. It looked right. It felt right. It was as if it had been missing all these years.

"I wish you luck on your tour and pray that you come back safely," Judge Street said as he shook my hand.

"Thank you, sir."

"I wish you a long and happy marriage," he directed his words toward Prue. She had only said what was necessary during our vows and nothing more.

She spoke softly meeting his eyes. "Thank you, sir."

PRUE'S SILENCE WAS GOING TO KILL ME. WE WERE headed back to her house after visiting a lawyer in Riverside, and she hadn't said a single word since speaking to the judge. The lawyer who handled my inheritance had FedExed the paperwork that needed to be signed. In less than a month, Prue would have more money than she knew what to do with and would also be debt free.

She hadn't read the paperwork. Not one word. She signed on the dotted line half a dozen times and then folded her hands in her lap while I spoke to the lawyer. It was like she was in a trance. I was afraid she already regretted marrying me. But really, I had no idea what was going on in that head of hers. The only thing I knew was that she was sad.

Pulling up in front of her house, I shut off the ignition and turned toward her. I wanted to touch her again. To pull her into my arms and never let her go, but I knew my advances wouldn't be welcome.

"Are you okay?" I finally asked after another few moments of her staring out the window.

"I'll be okay," she croaked out and then cleared her throat.

At least she admitted she wasn't fine.

"Do you want to talk about it?" I asked even though I knew she wouldn't tell me. At least, not yet. I knew I had a lot of work to do before she'd open up to me and trust me again.

"I should…" She paused, lifting her head to look at her house. Tears filled her eyes. "I don't even know what to do anymore. Who am I? I'm so used to working and taking care of my dad and now I don't do either of those things. What do I do?" she shakily questioned.

"You can do whatever you want to do. Find yourself. Find what makes you *you* now. Look for a new house and then decorate it. Travel. Be happy."

"I don't know, Holden. It doesn't feel right spending your money." She glanced my way, her face still sad.

"What's mine is yours. We're married now. Trust me, you don't need to worry about it. There's no way for you to possibly ever spend all the money I just inherited."

A sudden look of shock passed across her beautiful face. "I had no idea that your grandfather was that rich. I can't believe you walked away from all that money before."

"It was easy to do when they threatened your schooling," I responded truthfully.

"I had no idea," she whispered, her eyes large with astonishment.

"I only ask for one thing," I amended, unable to look at her. I was afraid of what I'd see when I asked.

"Of course, you do." I could hear the eye roll in her tone which made me crack a smile.

"I want…it gets lonely overseas. Since I've been estranged from my family, I have no one but the guys in my squad. I only ask that I can write you and get to know you again. Become friends. And that maybe you'll write me back."

"That's not what I was expecting," she whispered, brows pulled together. "I…you can write to me. I'm so confused by everything that's happened this week. From my dad dying to you showing up unexpectedly, and now we're married." She shook her head, looking out the window. "It's unbelievable, and I think I must still be in shock. I'm still mad at you, Holden. So, so angry. You have no idea." Fresh tears shimmered in her eyes. "I needed you and you were gone."

I swallowed the lump in my throat and held myself

back from reaching out to her. "I wish I had been there for you, but I'm here for you now if you'll let me. You only have to let me in."

"I already did that once and look how that turned out. I'm not sure I can do it again."

7

WHY WAS I SO SAD HOLDEN WAS GONE? I SHOULD HAVE been used to him being out of my life. *Why had I let him into my heart even the tiniest amount? Why hadn't I pushed him away when I had the chance?*

I spent my wedding night alone, crying in bed, and the worst part about it was the hopelessness in Holden's eyes when I got out of his car and walked away. I felt like a huge bitch hurting Holden even if I was only stating the truth. I couldn't promise him that I'd let him in. Not after all the pain he'd put me through.

Maybe I should have asked him to come in and fixed us dinner so we could hash out what it meant to be married now. But I didn't want to have to talk to him. Every time I was around him, my emotions were all over the place. I felt like I was on a rollercoaster the entire time he was in any proximity to me. One minute,

I was sad. The next angry. I wasn't going to lie; there were times when he made me forget about our past and my dad, which only ignited the rollercoaster once everything came crashing back down.

It had been a little over a month since we'd gotten married and Holden had left. He'd said goodbye from inside the car and then drove away. The look that was in his eyes haunted me every night in my dreams. I wasn't sure what it meant, but it felt like he thought he'd never see me again. I hadn't heard a word from him until today when I received a letter in the mail. I hadn't read it yet because I was a coward. Afraid of what it might say and what it might not. It taunted me with his tiny script spelling out my name on the envelope, reminding me of all the notes he'd written me in high school.

With shaking hands, I slowly opened his letter.

DEAR PRUE,

It's been one week since I left you, although from what I hear from the guys here, you probably won't get my letter for close to a month if not longer. I hope that one day you'll give me your email address, and we can write that way, or I can write you, and then it won't take so long to get to you. I hate knowing if you write to me it might take me a month to read what you have to say.

As I said before, I left, I'm hoping to get to know you again and praying that one day you'll forgive me for leaving and not speaking to you. I hope you know that I only left because I loved you more than anything and couldn't let my parents ruin your future. Your dreams. When I went back to talk to you and you were gone, I knew I had royally fucked up. I checked to see if you were around the campus of Loyola but turned up nothing. I had no idea where to look for you. Then it took even more time for me to save up enough money to hire a private investigator and for him to find you.

I wish you knew how terribly sorry I am for leaving you and not being there for you when you needed me most. That I wasn't there for you when you found out your dad was sick or to help take care of you while you took care of him. I would give anything to turn back time and fix us.

I hate that you felt you needed to move to get away from all the memories of us. If you're like me, I'm not sure you succeeded because there's not a day that's gone by that I haven't thought of you. You're in my thoughts constantly. I'm always wondering what you're doing or if you're okay. Even more so now after seeing you. But I understand how hard it would be to turn a corner or walk into a store and remember. We were so good together, and I ruined us.

By now you should have the money to pay off all your bills, and I hope you've done so. You don't need that stress on top of losing your father. I hope each day losing him becomes a little bit easier. Except losing you, I've never lost anyone close to me, so I can't speak from experience, but at least I knew you were alive. As *you know, I had only met my grandfather once, and then he passed away.*

I know you didn't agree to write me, but on the off chance that you will or someday will, here's some questions to help me get to know you better if you choose to answer.

I know you said you moved away, so where did you go to nursing school at?

Did you finish nursing school (because if not you can always go back)?

Are you still in contact with anyone from back home?

Have you started looking for a house?

I don't want to bombard you with too many questions, so I'll stop there. If you do write me back, please feel free to ask me anything and I promise to answer. My email is holdenmont-gomery@mail.mil.

All the Best,
Holden

TEARS SPLASHED FREELY ONTO THE PAPER I STILL HELD loosely in my hand. Deep down under all his muscles and ink, Holden was still the sweet boy I used to love. I could see him in there when he'd been here, and after reading his letter, I was even more convinced. But how could I get over him breaking my heart? How could I forgive him for making a decision that drastically changed both our lives? How could I forgive him for leaving me?

Did I want to forgive him?

I had never been a person who craved tension or conflict. I was easy going about almost everything in my life except for Holden. I wasn't sure there was any going back after what he'd done. I wasn't sure if letting him into my life was going to mend the gaping hole he'd left or shatter the last pieces of my heart until I was completely broken.

I wasn't naïve. I knew that if I let him in even the smallest amount, Holden would consume me if I wasn't careful.

Not knowing what to do, I did nothing. I didn't write back. I didn't even think about Holden. Instead, I holed myself up in my room, under the covers, in total darkness.

8

Prue,

It's been about two weeks since I last wrote, and this is the first chance I've had to write again. One of the other teams…you don't need to know what happened to them, but damn it's got me scared. I knew those men and how meticulous they were about their safety. What if I don't make it home? What if I never see you again?

This is the first time I've truly been scared while here. Things are not good here. Each time we go out, we're out longer and longer. Once we get back, it isn't long until we're sent out again. I'm not sure if they show an accurate depiction of what's going on here on the news. I doubt it though because anyone who had friends and/or family here would be freaking out.

I'm sorry. I don't want you to worry. That's not what this is *about. I just want to talk to you. To be able to tell someone how I'm feeling and get it out of my system. I know you didn't believe me, but I swear you've been in my thoughts all these years. You're still the most important person in my life and knowing how much pain I caused you keeps me up at night.*

I don't mean to pressure you, but please write me back. Even if it's only to tell me to fuck off. Let me know how you're doing. When I left, you were so despondent. If I could have come at a better time I would have, but I couldn't stay away when I found out about your dad. I wish I could have done more for you, but I understand why you wouldn't let me. Fuck, Prue, I'm so sorry. I miss you so much. I hope you're doing better.

All My Best,
Holden

P.S.
Have you found a house?

9

To: *holdenmontgomery@mail.mil*
From: *nurseprue@gmail.com*
Subject: *Email Address*

Holden,

I'm still upset. I can't help it, but it kills me to know that you're
over there and scared for your life. I don't want you to have to wait
a month to receive a letter from me so here I am, and I'm trying.
If you need to talk, I'm here for you.

Prue

To: *nurseprue@gmail.com*

From: holdenmontgomery@mail.mil
Subject: Thank You!

Prue,

You have no idea how much it means to me that you gave me your email address and to hear from you. Even those few words were enough. I needed something good to happen in my life today. I wish I was back in your little town with you, begging you to forgive me for being a stupid idiot. I wish I would have talked to you before I left after graduation. I have so many things I wish I could do over in my life.

I've had a lot of time to think over the past few years and after seeing you again, I think I know why you were so sad on that last day. I mean, I know you were sad about your dad, but I didn't do right by you. I know I didn't. Never did you imagine getting married by judge without any friends or family there. It wasn't your dream wedding. How could it have been? If it makes you feel any better, it means more to me than you know and not because of the money. I don't give a shit about the money. The only things in the world I care about are getting out of here alive and you. I only hope one day you'll believe me and give me a chance.

Sometimes when I miss home, I sit outside and look up at the stars and wonder if you're looking at them too. I know it's not

logical because of the time difference, but it helps me. If you ever
need me, look up at the stars, and I'll be there. At least in spirit.

I have to go. Duty calls, but I hope to hear from you soon.

Holden

To: holdenmontgomery@mail.mil
From: nurseprue@gmail.com
Subject: Re: Thank You!

Holden,

I hope you're okay. I don't watch much TV and if I do it's not
the news. It's too depressing. There's too much violence and polit-
ical bullshit in the world. I have to admit, you have me worried.
Despite my being mad at you, I don't want anything bad to
happen to you. You have to come home so I can properly scream
and yell at you when I'm not in shock. You can email me any
time, and I promise to read and try to answer them. You had some
questions before and here are your answers.

Yes, I finished nursing school. When we moved, I enrolled in a
fast track two-year program. Before I had to take leave and got
fired, I worked at a local doctor's office. I really miss working

there. I enjoyed my co-workers and the patients. I haven't found a new job yet, but I've been looking at houses. I asked my friend Alex what neighborhood she lived in, and you would not believe what she told me. It's a neighborhood owned by Colton Patrick. Did you know he's from Fairlane? Crazy enough, she met him before she met Luke. Anyway, Alex has helped me look some when she's had the time. I'll let you know if I find one.

I don't talk to anyone back home. The only person I talk to is my old neighbor, Alex. I know it's sad, but I didn't have the time with how sick my dad got or the money to do anything. But that's okay because I wouldn't trade the time I spent with my dad for anything in the world.

Can you tell me where you are over there?

Do you have many friends there? I know you said it gets lonely.

Prue

10

To: nurseprue@gmail.com
From: holdenmontgomery@mail.mil
Subject: Don't Worry
Date: March 4, 2018 9:39 pm

Prue,

Don't be worried about me. I'm sorry I can't tell you much, not that I'd want to. The more you know the more you'd worry. We are at war here, and we have to stay vigilant about our safety.

Again, I hate that you felt the need to move, but I'm proud of you for becoming a nurse. Don't feel pressured to find a job. I know you don't want to sit around doing nothing all day, but I want you to find the right fit for you. Don't take anything just to have a job.

From what I hear, finding, buying, and decorating a house can be a job in and of itself.

Colton Patrick, the movie star? Wow! That's amazing. I had no idea he was from Fairlane. It's crazy he's from such a small town, and now you're living there. Not to mention your neighbor knows him.

After shutting out my parents and finding out you were no longer in town, I had no reason to keep in touch with anyone. They were all off to college, and none of them were the type to write. I didn't mind though. You were/are the only one I cared about.

I'm friends with the guys in my squad. Luckily, we all get along, but we don't really talk about deep stuff much. Sometimes there are occasions that require it, but normally we try to keep it on the light side for obvious reasons. There are a couple of guys who will always be my brothers though. We've been through some shit, and it has created a bond that can't be broken. We're family and nothing can change that. On our downtime, we play video games, poker, read, and sleep. Mostly we sleep to catch up on all the hours we miss while we're out.

Thank you for writing me back. It was the first time I've smiled since I got here. It feels like I've got a little bit of you back. Please don't let that scare you off. Right now, you're the only bright light in my otherwise dark world.

All the Best,

Holden

To: holdenmontgomery@mail.mil

From: nurseprue@gmail.com

Subject: Don't tell me not to worry

Date: March 12, 2018 9:08 am

Holden,

I wish the world knew how difficult it is over there and how much all of you sacrifice for our country. You tell me not to worry, but I can't help it. I know it might not seem like it, but I do care for you. I always have and there's nothing that can stop me.

Even if you're safe, which it doesn't sound as if you are, you seem to be in a very dark place. Did something happen? You used to be so easy going and upbeat, and now, I hate to say it, but that seems to be gone. If you can't tell me, I understand. I know there's lots you can't say.

I think I might have found a house. I love it, but it's way too big for me. I know you said I could buy anything, but it feels silly when it's just me. So, I'm thinking about getting a dog. I've been so lonely without my dad. I don't know what to do with myself.

Alex has been busy with her new house, her son, and work. She works like crazy even now when she doesn't have to. Right now, she's in LA visiting Luke, and when he moves here in a couple of months, I doubt I'll see her much. I understand, though, since she's gone so long without much time with him.

Seeing her in love makes my heart happy and gives me hope that one day I can have that too. I probably shouldn't be telling you this, but we're friends, right? That's what we've been working toward. I thought it would take longer for me, but damn you, Holden, you've worked your way under my skin. I hope that you didn't make me worry about you because you knew it would soften my heart to you. But even writing that, I know you didn't.

No matter what, if you need me, I'm here for you.

Prue

To: nurseprue@gmail.com
From: holdenmontgomery@mail.mil
Subject: Buy It!
Date: March 13, 2018 1:08 am

Prue,

I don't care how big the house is. Even if it has thirty bedrooms. Buy it! You can always fill them up with puppies and children. Hopefully, my children. Yeah, I went there, and I'm sorry if you're not ready to hear it, but you are 'my one.' You're it for me. I've known since the moment I saw you in the school parking lot. I know that it doesn't seem like it when I up and left you, but I was a stupid kid who was trying to do right by you. I had to tell you when you mentioned about hoping to find love after seeing your friend in love. I'm hoping that you can love me again and give me a chance.

I know I've already pushed too much as it is, but do you think we can get to the point where we can Skype? Do you have an account? I would love to be able to hear your voice and see your beautiful face. Think about it.

I've got to go, and it will be at least a couple of days before I can get back to you. Since I've never written anyone while here, I didn't think about it, but I wanted to let you know that sometimes we're in a blackout and can't send or receive any type of communication. So, if it takes a while to hear from me that's why.

All the Best,
Holden

11

PRUE

To: holdenmontgomery@mail.mil
From: nurseprue@gmail.com
Subject: Skype
Date: March 15, 2018 10:12 pm

Holden,

Was I ready for that? No, I definitely wasn't, but I want you to be able to say anything you want to me. Most of the time, I hate that you're all the way across the world from me, but I know that if you were here, I'd still be so angry at you and pushing you away. For that, I'm thankful as bad as it sounds.

Since I'm being so honest with you, I've got to confess you made me cry with your last email. Back in high school, I had our kids' names picked out, and for you to say you hoped even now we

*would have kids someday opened up those old wounds. I know I
need to get over the hurt, and I am. Slowly but surely. Each letter
and email shows me my old Holden is still in that big body of
yours, and I know you regret leaving. Like you said, I can be stubborn. I promise one day I'll forgive you and be over our past.*

*On to lighter subjects: I'm going to go back and look at the house I
like next week when Alex gets back from LA. I haven't found
another house I like nearly as much. It's just so big! I won't need
a job because I'll spend all my time cleaning the house.*

*I'm going to set up a Skype account tomorrow so we can talk.
When I see you again, I'll know if I'm over being angry or not.
Does that make any sense? You said it would be a few days before
you would get back to me. You'll be in my thoughts and prayers
until I know you're safe.*

Prue

*P.S.
What does a blackout mean?*

*To: holdenmontgomery@mail.mil
From: nurseprue@gmail.com
Subject: Hello?*

Date: March 20, 2018 11:59 pm

Holden,

I know you said it would be a few days, but it's been a week since your last email. If there's any way possible for you to even say hi please do so. I need to know you're okay.

I set up my Skype account and my name is nurseprue just like my email.

I hope to hear from you soon.

Prue

To: holdenmontgomery@mail.mil
From: nurseprue@gmail.com
Subject: Officially Worried
Date: March 23, 2018 10:48 pm

Holden,

If I knew who to call to find out any information about you, I would have called them a million times by now. If something happened to you, I'll never forgive you. I can't buy the house until

I know you're okay. Please write me back. Do something to let me know you're still alive.

Prue

To: nurseprue@gmail.com
From: holdenmontgomery@mail.mil
Subject: Re: Officially Worried
Date: March 25, 2018 3:25 am

Prue,
I'm alive and so fucking tired. After I get some sleep, I'll try to Skype you.

Talk to you soon,
Holden

IF ANYONE WOULD HAVE TOLD ME THREE YEARS AGO, OR even three months ago, that I would be happy to hear from Holden, I would have laughed in their face. After getting his email, I danced around the house, smiled, and laughed for the first time in months. Then I sat around my laptop all day hoping to hear from him again. As each passing hour went by, I started to worry again, but then had to remind myself there were many things that could prevent Holden from contacting me. He had other things to do that were more important than me.

Not giving up, I took my laptop into my bedroom and set it up on my nightstand. I wasn't going to miss Holden contacting me because I had to get some sleep. For the past several days, I'd barely slept from worry and my imagination running away with me on what could have possibly happened to him.

For the first time since Holden had left me, I was happy that for the past three years I hadn't gone through the torture of waiting for him to call and worrying about him incessantly. I wasn't sure how military spouses did it for years on end because I'd only been doing it for a short while, and I was a nervous wreck most of the time. All I knew was that they were strong beyond belief.

As I laid my head on my pillow and hoped sleep would find me, my computer started doing it's Do Dee Do Blup Blup Blup Do Dee Do Blup Blup Blup thing.

Sitting up with a giant grin on my face, I grabbed my computer and hit the video button. My eyes widened at the sight of Holden on my screen. He looked older than he had only a couple of months ago.

"Hey," I called out happily.

The smile died on my face when Holden leaned forward to touch the screen with tears in his eyes. "Prue," he choked out, his face almost touching the screen.

"I'm here. Talk to me."

His eyes darted around taking me in, but he didn't say a word as his face crumpled, and he broke down half a world away.

"Are you okay?" My nose started to tingle, and my eyes burned.

First nodding and then shaking his head, Holden took in a deep breath and composed himself. "You look beautiful," he said hoarsely.

Blushing, I murmured a thank you and tried to smile, but the look on Holden's face churned something deep inside of me. Something was wrong, and I had a feeling I wasn't going to be successful in getting him to talk about it.

"I hate to be rude, but you don't look so good. Since I last saw you, you've lost weight and you look so tired. Talk to me. Tell me what's happening with you."

"No," he shook his head and closed his eyes. "I just need to hear your voice." He opened his eyes with hope shining brightly back at me. "Tell me what's going on with you. Did you buy the house?"

I let out a breath. I knew it was a long shot for him to tell me what had happened. I wanted to help him if

I could, and if talking to him about my mundane life helped, I would do it.

"Not yet. I've been out of my mind worried about you. I couldn't buy a house thinking the worst had happened to you." Shit, that wasn't helping matters, but it was the truth.

"I'm sorry, Prue. I got back to you as soon as I could. I always will. Sometimes it just takes a little longer." He smiled sadly at me. "Tell me about the house."

"I know nothing about houses and styles and all that, but the moment I stepped inside, I loved it. It feels like home. It has exposed beams everywhere and huge windows with gorgeous views. It has a few acres behind it that are filled with trees and even a little stream. It has five bedrooms, a den, and three fireplaces. There's one in the living room and master bedroom, and then there's one outside. Can you believe that?"

"It sounds perfect," he smiled softly.

"It really is. You can change your mind if you want. You really don't have to buy me a house. I'm thankful enough that you paid off my student loans and all my dad's medical bills."

"No, Prue," he sat up straighter. "I want to do this for you. Buy the house. I don't care how much it is or how big. Remember, you can always fill it up."

"With puppies and babies," I whispered.

"How do you feel about that?" He swallowed hard, his Adam's apple bobbing.

I bit my bottom lip and asked. "Truthfully?"

"Always," he promised.

Sucking in a deep breath, I looked Holden over. Even from half a world away, he was still handsome. The chocolatey eyes I'd always loved looked as if they'd seen too much. He was haunted and slightly broken, and I wanted desperately to fix him.

"Right now, I'm only ready for one puppy, but in the future, I hope for more." I smiled weakly, trying to reassure him. "I wish you could see the house so I could get your opinion on it."

"You don't need my opinion. Stop second guessing yourself. You love it, and that's all that matters."

"Do you feel any better?" I asked unable to hide the hope in my voice.

"Yeah, listening to you and seeing your face," he nodded more to himself than me, "it helps after a hard few days. I'm sorry I scared you." He looked down for a moment, and when he looked up, his eyes were clouded over with pain.

"I wish I were there to hug you." The words barely formed around the lump in my throat. Tears stung the backs of my eyes, but I held them back. Holden didn't need to see me cry. I needed to be strong for him.

"I wish that too. More than you know. I've been

thinking about what I'm going to do once I get out of the military."

"Oh, yeah? Have you decided on anything?"

"Not really. I can do whatever I want, and I have no idea what that is," he shook his head dejectedly.

"Do you still want to be an architect? You have the money to go to school and do whatever you want."

"Won't I be too old to go to college?" he asked with a disheartening laugh.

"No," I waved that idea away, "you can go to college at any age. I mean, you probably won't be asked to join any fraternities, but there are plenty of people who go back to school or start school late."

He laughed, and my world brightened. "I don't think I could put up with a bunch of drunk frat guys and the party scene."

"When you're done, take your time figuring out what you want to do. You'll figure it out. I bet you could use a nice, relaxing vacation."

"Could I come there and visit you?" He swallowed nervously.

"If you want," I answered back just as nervous.

"More than anything." He looked off to the side and frowned. "I've got to go. I promised my buddy he could use my computer. If I sent a list of things, would you send them to me?"

"Of course, I would," I answered without thought.

"Does this mean you're no longer mad at me?" His eyes brightened at the thought.

"I guess it does. I'm not mad anymore. Just worried about you. Promise me something, Holden. If you can't or won't talk to me, talk to someone. Can you do that for me?"

Holden looked down for a moment. I used to always know if he lied to me. Was he preparing to lie to me now? "How about if I promise you that I'll try?"

"Is that the best I'll get?"

"It's the best I can do right now," he promised.

"Okay, that's all I can ask of you."

"Thanks, Prue. Talking to you...helped. I l... I'll talk to you soon."

Then he disconnected. The screen was blank where he once had been, and instantly, I missed him.

Had Holden been about to tell me he loved me? More importantly, was Holden okay? Gone was the sweet boy I used to know, and in his place was someone I barely recognized.

After a few letters and one video chat, Holden had wormed his way back into my heart. He wanted there to be an us again, but would he break my heart if I let him back into my life? But hadn't I already let him back in? I had a feeling Holden needed me more now than ever before, and whatever we were doing was going to get a lot harder before it ever got better.

12

To: nurseprue@gmail.com
From: holdenmontgomery@mail.mil
Subject: Thanks
Date: May 5, 2018 4:47 am

Prue,

Thank you! I got my package. You went well above what I asked for. Hell, you supplied the whole unit, and now they all love you. I'm constantly being harassed to show them a picture of you. Not in a million years am I going to share what you look like. Then you'll have a squad of stalkers. Even if half of them are married.

I know you're busy moving, but I had to write you after I got your package earlier to let you know I finally received it. I wanted you to know, I guess it takes even longer to get packages and for you not to worry. For the time being, I'm back sleeping and playing video games with the guys. One thing I'm not sharing is the food you sent. I've already eaten one of everything. Thank you again!

I hope the move goes well. Let me know when you get settled.

All the Best,
Holden

To: holdenmontgomery@mail.mil
From: nurseprue@gmail.com
Subject: You're Welcome
Date: May 7, 2018 9:35 pm

Holden,

I'm finally finished moving. Well, I still have stuff to unpack, but the house is livable, and that's what matters. I only have time on my hands, so I'm not rushing the process. I'm wiped out and about ready to head to bed in a few minutes, but I wanted to write you a quick message.

I'm glad you got your package. I knew that if you could, you'd give all your guys packages, so I only did what you would have done. I'm glad everyone is enjoying them. Who knew new socks were such a luxury? Certainly not me. I'm not sure how well-preserved the food I sent is since it took so long to get there. I guess candy bars don't go bad that easily. If you want me to send you anything else that will make your time over there easier, please let me know. Up until the move, I've been getting kind of bored and lonely, so I was happy to have a mission. And happy to help you in any way that I can. I'm going to go look at a litter of puppies next weekend. By then, I should have pretty much everything unpacked, or so I hope.

Did I tell you that Alex is spending the whole summer in Hawaii? Luke is filming a movie there and asked her and Mason to join him. I'm a little jealous. I've always wanted to go.

Talk to you soon,
Prue

13

PRUE

Do Dee Do Blup Blup Blup Do Dee Do Blup Blup Blup

I ran to my computer and hit video, plopping down on my bed.

"Hey," I greeted Holden, slightly out of breath.

His answering smile was enough for me. It took some time, and I never found out what had Holden so upset, but it seemed he was finally out of his funk. It was nice getting to know him again. Much was the same, and he still didn't want to talk about the things that weren't. I wasn't sure if it was because I'd gotten worried when he couldn't contact me, and he didn't want me to become more worried, or if he couldn't talk about it. Either way, I wasn't going to pressure him. If he ever wanted to talk, I would be there for him.

"Did you go look at the dogs today?" he asked, resting his face on his hand.

"I did," I knew I had a dreamy look on my face as I sighed thinking about all the cute puppies. "I don't know how I could possibly choose just one. I wanted to bring them all home."

"Well, you have the room," he laughed.

"That I do, but I don't want to have to potty train that many puppies."

"Did they finish the fence or is it still raining?"

"The fence is finally finished. I thought it was never going to stop raining." I pulled the computer further up the bed and laid down.

With brows furrowed, he asked worriedly. "Shit, Prue, did I call too late?"

"It's not too late. I just wanted to get comfortable. You look like you got some good sleep."

"A little." He smiled shyly. "Why do you have that look on your face that means you're keeping something from me?"

I didn't want to tell him, but I knew I couldn't lie to Holden. Yet, I couldn't get it out of my head either. "Holden, how would you feel if I told you that someone asked me out today when I was at the grocery store?"

I'd barely gotten the sentence out before his face

turned red, and he looked as if he might explode at any moment. I think I got my answer.

"I wouldn't be fucking happy, for sure. Why would some guy ask you out? Do you not wear your wedding ring?"

"How am I supposed to know why some guy would ask me out?"

Holden growled with his eyes narrowed on the screen.

"Do you wear your ring?" I returned the question. I had no idea if he wore his or not. We hadn't talked about anything but getting married, paying off my debt, and buying a house. I didn't know at the time if he planned to date during our marriage or what.

"Yes, Prue," he barked out, holding his left hand up showing his wedding band on his finger. "I do wear mine. The real question is, do you?"

"Why are you getting mad at me?"

"Because you're telling me that while I'm all the way over here, guys are asking you out! If you were wearing your rings, I don't think that would happen," he growled out.

"Well, for your information, I do wear them. But you know what, Holden, we didn't talk about what this marriage would mean."

"Would mean?" he interrupted. "Did you plan to date and screw guys through our entire marriage?"

"See, that right there is why we should have had a prenup or not have gotten married in the first place."

"I was trying to fucking help you," he growled loudly. I could feel the vibration through the computer.

I sat up, furious. "So, now you're going to hold it over my head? I don't think so," I spat. "I'll sell the fucking house, and I don't care if it takes me the rest of my life, I will pay you back every dime. I don't need you or your help."

"Yes, you fucking do. I thought you'd hold our vows sacred," he said the last words and his expression evolved from anger to hurt.

"Oh my God, this is why we should have talked."

"I guess so," he hissed.

"Are you telling me you've been celibate?"

"Of course, I have." He looked at me as if I'd lost my mind. "Do you think I've turned gay? I'm literally around men twenty-four-seven."

"Are you saying that if you were around women, you'd be having sex with them?" I grated out.

"Where are you getting these ideas?" he asked, eyes wide with bewilderment. "Is it because you've been dating and having sex?"

"Yes, Holden, that's exactly what I'm saying. While I've been grieving for my father, I've been out whoring around. I thought you knew me better than that."

"It's obvious we don't know each other at all anymore," he barked.

"Obviously, I'm done with this." I threw my hands up. "Let me know what you decide. I can put the house up on the market tomorrow."

"Why are you always so damn stubborn?" he shot back. "The house is yours. Stop trying to give it back."

"Stop being an asshole and jumping to conclusions."

"I only know what you tell me, Prue. Why bring up a guy asking you out if you didn't want to make me jealous and piss me off?"

"You fucking asked," I accused. "I… I felt weird that he asked me out. I can barely remember the last time someone asked me out. For you to insinuate that…" I shook my head, tears building.

"I know you're not a whore, Prue," he murmured, his eyes softening.

"Do you?" I snapped. "It certainly doesn't seem like it. Why don't you tell me how many women you've had sex with since you left town?"

He blanched, and I wanted to be sick. I knew it was wrong for me to expect Holden to not have had sex in all the years he'd been gone. Why did it matter? We weren't together, although he certainly acted like we were. I didn't understand what he wanted from me. Yes, Holden had hinted at wanting more from me than friendship, but that was the thing, it was just a hint. We hadn't talked about it since then. I needed to stay strong. I couldn't open myself up to him only for him to leave me in the dust and licking my wounds in two years. I had a feeling this time there would be nothing left of me.

"Prue, calm down. I don't have much time, and I don't want to fight over some misunderstanding." He took a deep breath and closed his eyes. When they opened back up, they were filled with determination. "Look, I know I wasn't been very forthcoming with what I wanted or expected before I deployed, and I know I hurt you immensely when I left after graduation. That's an understatement. I know because it nearly killed me to leave you, and when I came back, you were gone." The pain he felt back then reflected in his eyes, making me feel my own. "I tried to convince myself it was for the best, but trust me, it wasn't easy leaving you. I've had to live with myself knowing that I broke your heart.

"For the rest of my life, I will beg you to forgive me, to tell you how fucking sorry I am, because I *am* so fucking sorry. Every time I see your face, I'm reminded of making the worst mistake of my life. But then when you smile at me, I think I just might have a shot of winning you back. Because that's what I plan to do if you'll give me a chance," he implored.

"Not once in all these years have I stopped loving you. Not for one moment. And there have been times when I've prayed that I could stop so maybe the ache in my heart would go away for even the tiniest amount of time, but how could I stop loving you when you were —*are* the best thing that's ever happened to me? I couldn't. It's impossible, so I resigned myself to a fate of always being alone with a broken heart." He shook his head, laughing bitterly.

"That's where I'm at. I want you for forever. If you'll have me. I told you we could divorce in two years, but only so you'd agree to marry me. I planned to have you so in love with me by that time that you'd never want to leave. I knew you'd never agree to marry me if you knew I never planned to let you go."

My mind was blown. Never did I expect any of this. From the time we'd started talking again, this was the most Holden had said. Normally, he let me do all the talking. He encouraged it actually.

"Your life. My life. It's all up to you. If you tell me to stay away and to leave you alone, then I will, but I really hope you won't. I need you, Prue. Not that I'm trying to guilt you into anything, but now you know how I feel."

"Holden," I choked out his name in half prayer, half cursing him, "I don't know what to say."

"Say you'll think about it. Really think about all I've

said and search deep down in your heart for what you want. That's all I can ask, and once you decide, I promise that I'll respect your decision."

"You make it sound so easy." I wanted so badly to cry in that moment.

"If I have to let you go, it will be the hardest thing I've ever had to do. I did it once, and it nearly killed me. I…"

"I promise to think about it," I interrupted him, afraid of what he might say next. "About everything you've said. Who's to say you won't want to leave me when the two years are up or even when you get back," I confessed my fear.

"I say," he vowed.

"It's not that simple," I argued.

"It is that simple. I know myself, and I know what I've felt and wanted for almost four years. I'm not going to change my mind. Don't you want *me* anymore?" he asked the last on a whisper.

"You might change your mind once you have me," I managed to get out. "I can't go through you leaving me again. I won't survive it."

"Prue," he called out with pain searing me from his soulful eyes, "I promise if you give yourself to me, I won't ever let you go. When I said my vows, I meant every word of them."

"I…" My throat clogged up, unable to answer.

"You don't have to answer right now. I've given you a lot to think about. You had no idea I was feeling this way, and I'm sure it's a shock to you."

"It is, but in a good way."

"I want you to be Mrs. Montgomery. To be my wife."

"I already am," I giggled.

"I want those things with you because you want them with me. Think about it for a couple of days. They're sending us out again, but I'll call you when I get back. If you don't hear from me for a few days, don't be worried. When someone dies or gets severely injured here, they blackout all communication until they can contact the family. It's frustrating, but we understand. I know you wanted to know what a blackout means and now you know."

"In a way that helps unless it's you." I laughed sadly. "Every time you tell me you're out there where the bad guys are, I'm always worried. Just because you tell me not to isn't going to change that."

"Fair enough. Although I do wish you wouldn't worry about me..." He looked off to the side and tensed. "Shit, I gotta go. I'll talk to you soon. I love you."

And then he disconnected without letting me say anything back. He'd said I love you so easily, and I didn't even know if I could have said anything in response. It didn't matter because he hadn't given me the chance.

All I knew was that I had a lot of soul searching to do.

Could I give Holden my heart again?

14

To: holdenmontgomery@mail.mil
From: nurseprue@gmail.com
Subject: I Want You
Date: June 11, 2018 6:11 am

Holden,

I want you. I want you so damn much it hurts that you're not here with me. I hate that I can't tell you in person, but I couldn't wait. So, you better not break my heart again. I couldn't sleep last night. My mind replayed everything you said on a loop. I realized that I'd always regret not giving you a chance. You've always been my one true love, and how can I throw that away? I can't. Plain and simple.

I wanted you to know as soon as you got back. I can't wait to see your handsome face again.

Today I'm going to pick out a puppy. I'm not sure if they'll let me bring one home today or not. I hope so, that way my mind will be on something other than you out on a mission and worried about you.

I hope to hear from you soon.

All My Love,
Prue

To: holdenmontgomery@mail.mil
From: nurseprue@gmail.com
Subject: I'm a Mother
Date: June 13, 2018 9:39 am

Holden,

If you couldn't guess from the subject, they let me bring home a puppy! He is the cutest and sweetest thing ever. He's a mini Australian Shepherd and Pomeranian mix. I love him already, but how could you not with his big puppy dog eyes and sweet puppy breath? His name is Atticus, and I know you're going to fall in love with him when you finally get to meet him.

Waiting to hear from you.

All My Love,
Prue

15

PRUE

THE WEATHER HAD BEEN BAD FOR THE PAST TWO WEEKS, and Atticus and I needed supplies. I was down to the last can of soup, so when it finally stopped raining and flooding, I decided to venture out to go shopping. I hated to leave Atticus locked up in his crate, but I didn't know how long I'd be gone and didn't want to find pee spots all over the floor once I got home. I headed to Riverside because Fairlane's shopping options were so limited. Riverside had a PetSmart and Target along with a Trader Joe's to get all my shopping needs completed. The only problem was that it was a little over thirty minutes away from my house, and when I finally finished shopping, the sky had darkened drastically. I thought the rain was done for the foreseeable future, but I guess I'd been wrong. There was a river running through the parking lot, but I thought nothing of it. I was ready to get home, put everything away, curl up on the couch, and read a book. Hopefully, later I'd hear from Holden, but I wasn't holding my breath. I was barely a mile down the road when the sky opened up, and the road instantly flooded. The water rushed over my windshield, making it even more difficult to see. Turning my windshield wipers on high, I drove carefully, trying to stay away from the side of the road; the water that had built up in the undercarriage of my car threatened to overtake my steering.

Not everyone on the road was as concerned for themselves or others, and I got nervous when I saw more than one car pulled off on the side of the road before passing a three-car pile-up. I was used to driving in bad weather and rain, but I couldn't see two feet in front of me. In most places, there wasn't a shoulder big enough for a car to pull off the road without potentially going over the side into the steep ditch. Each time I found an open shoulder with enough space, another car would take the spot before I had a chance to pull over, leaving me frustrated and concerned.

Distracted and nervous, I was focused on pulling over and not on the cars on the other side of the road coming toward me. My eyes flashed up and to the side when a blaring horn caught my attention. From the other side, a large truck had lost control and was headed right for the car in front of me. All my driving sense flew out the window; I slammed on the brakes in panic. My car fishtailed, and when I tried to correct it, I realized I had put myself right in the trajectory of the truck that was now barreling toward me.

All I could do was brace myself as tires screeched and horns blared. It all seemed to happen in slow motion. When the truck hit the driver side of my crappy Ford Taurus, my head snapped back as my seatbelt dug into my skin and the airbag deployed in my face. Glass shattered, cutting into my exposed skin. When I opened my eyes, my vision was blurry, and as I tried to rub them to see better, my fingers came away red. Blood. There was blood everywhere.

I exhaled and my eyes blinked heavily. All I wanted to do was sleep. Each blink took a little longer to achieve.

"Miss, can you hear me? Can you tell me your first name?" Someone yanked away the seatbelt, searing my skin.

"Prue," I rasped out.

"Prue, we're here to help you. You're going to be fine. We're going to take you to the hospital. Do you know what happened?"

Strong hands lifted me from the car; pain shot through me as gravity pulled on my injured body. "Wreck."

"Yes, you were in a wreck. Please don't try to move.

We need to keep you stable until we've determined nothing is broken."

Bright lights shone above me. My eyes drifted closed, no longer able to stay open as the gentle sway of the ambulance rocked me to sleep—even as the EMT urged me to stay awake.

WHEN I WOKE UP, I WAS IN A HOSPITAL BED WITH A nurse taking my blood pressure.

"Good morning," she chirped. "How's our patient feeling today?"

Morning?

"What time is it?" I croaked out, my throat dry from misuse.

"A little after seven in the morning," she answered back with a sweet smile.

Shit! Poor Atticus had been home alone overnight. He was going to think I left him.

Sitting up, I tried to swing my legs off the bed but stopped when I got woozy.

"Miss, you need to lie back down. You've got a nasty bump on your head and a concussion." The nurse helped me lay back down and covered me up with a thin blanket, all the while watching me out of the corner of her eye.

"I need to get home. My dog's been alone since yesterday afternoon," I cried out weakly.

"Do you have anyone you can call to help take care of your dog until you're home?" She placed her hand on mine, smiling down at me.

"No one. My friend's out of town."

I had no one.

"What about your husband?" She patted my left hand, reminding me that I was indeed married.

But still alone.

"He's deployed," I started to shake my head but stopped as it started to throb.

"Well, God bless him and you. It must be tough being so young and separated."

She had no idea.

Tears trekked down my cheeks. I had no one to help me.

What if Holden was back and messaging me, and I wasn't answering him back? Would he be worried?

"Is my phone here?" I prayed I could call Alex, and she could somehow check my email.

"No, I'm sorry, but you can use the phone here if you know the number."

Who knew phone numbers anymore? And my head hurt too much to be able to remember anything. I was lucky I remembered my own name in that moment.

She must have seen something on my face because

she smiled sadly. "You should get some rest. Maybe then you'll remember the number."

Maybe.

"Everything will feel better with a little time and rest.

I certainly hoped so.

16

To: holdenmontgomery@mail.mil
From: nurseprue@gmail.com
Subject: Prue
Date: June 15, 2018 11:57 pm

Holden,

Hi. This is Alex, Prue's friend. Prue wanted me to let you know that she's okay, but she's in the hospital. Yesterday, she was in a pretty bad car accident from what she told me. I feel so bad that I can't be with her in Fairlane and help out, but we're in Hawaii for the summer. I offered to fly back, but she wouldn't have it. You know Prue. She hates asking for help and didn't want me to have to fly back and forth in only a few days. One of my friends offered to help with Atticus until she's out of the hospital and to take her home. He's very trustworthy, so I don't want you to worry, and I promise you he'll keep his hands to himself. Prue hasn't told me much about what's going on between you two, but I don't want you to torment yourself. I've known Josh since high school and trust him with my life.

Prue wanted me to also check and see if you'd messaged her back. She's been worried about you and hoped there'd be a message from you. Sadly, there's not, but I'll tell her not to worry. Although we both know that won't do any good. She should be home tonight or tomorrow morning and will probably email you yourself.

I know I don't know you, but thank you for putting the spark back in Prue's eyes. In all the time I've known her, I've never seen her so happy and hopeful. I hope to meet you when you get home.

Alex

I READ THE EMAIL AGAIN FOR THE THIRD TIME. PRUE was hurt and in the hospital, and there wasn't a single thing I could do to help her. Each day, I was closer to going home, but it wasn't soon enough. Most days, I needed Prue to make it through all the shit I'd seen. One look at her beautiful face, and I forgot everything but her. But she needed me, and I couldn't be there.

Not only could I not be there, but her friend was gone too. She must have felt so alone and scared.

I was almost tempted to call my parents and ask them to help, but I knew they wouldn't. If they knew I'd married Prue and had gotten my inheritance, they'd be livid, and who knew what they'd do. Prue didn't need them trying to make her life a living hell.

All I knew in that moment was that I'd give anything to be there with Prue. The only thing that got me through the days was knowing that she was going to give me a chance, and the fact that she still loved me after everything I'd put her through.

I wasn't sure if she would be home before I was sent out again. The only thing I could do was write her an email and hope to talk to her.

To: nurseprue@gmail.com
From: holdenmontgomery@mail.mil
Subject: Are You Okay?
Date: June 16, 2018 5:23 am

Prue,

God, you will never know how sorry I am that I can't be there for you. Your friend sent me an email letting me know you were in a wreck. Please tell me you're okay and let Alex's friend help you if you need it. Don't be so damn stubborn.

I can't think straight knowing that you're hurt and alone. Email me when you get home to let me know how you're doing.

If this is how you feel every time I tell you I'm being sent out, I don't know how you handle it. I hate not being able to talk to you. When you get home, I'm afraid it may be a few days before I can get back to you. We got word again that we were heading out sometime today or tomorrow. I'm supposed to be resting, but I know I'm not going to be able to sleep until I know you're home and okay.

I love you, Prue, and I'm sorry I've put us through so much pain over the years. I promise once I get home, I'm never going to cause you another ounce of pain for the rest of our lives.

Love,
Holden

To: nurseprue@gmail.com
From: holdenmontgomery@mail.mil
Subject: Please Be Okay
Date: June 16, 2018 10:38 am

Prue,

I know it's only been a few hours, but I needed to check my emails to see if you were home yet or had sent me a message. I hope you're home soon and feeling better. We're leaving in a couple of hours, and I have to get ready.
I want you to know you mean the world to me. You're the first thing I think of when I wake up and the last before I fall asleep. It's been that way since the day I met you. I'm still that love-sick teenager you met all those years ago.

Please message me as soon as you can, and I promise to do the same.

I love you,
Holden

17

To: holdenmontgomery@mail.mil
From: nurseprue@gmail.com
Subject: I'm Home
Date: June 16, 2018 4:23 pm

Holden,

You can stop worrying about me. I'm finally home. Alex's friend Josh even went to the grocery store for me since almost everything I bought was ruined after the wreck. He then went to where my car was towed and got Atticus' dog food. I'm so thankful for Alex contacting you and having Josh help me.

I know it will probably be a few days before you get this, but I know you were anxious to hear from me. I need to go though. I'm not supposed to be on the computer or watch TV or pretty much anything with my concussion. I guess I'll use this time to try to train Atticus. Skype me when you get back no matter the time. I'll keep my computer up and running.

Is it crazy that I miss you? Because I do. I know it's not fair to say this to you, but I wish you were here.

All My Love,
Prue

FOR THE PAST FEW DAYS, I'D DONE NOTHING BUT TRY TO train Atticus and failed. I'd bought a couple of videos to help me train him, but with my concussion, I couldn't watch them to learn what to do. Besides my failed attempt at dog training, I stared out the windows. I loved my view, but it did nothing to make me forget that Holden was out there fighting for our country, and there was a chance that he might not ever make it home to me.

Atticus was curled up against my side. He'd been dozing since our last round of 'sit' when my phone rang. Atticus' head lifted and his ears perked up. I smiled when I saw Alex's name flash across my screen.

"Hey," I answered.

"Hey, Prue. How are you?"

"Better but bored out of my mind. I can't even read."

"Really? What kind of bullshit is that?" She laughed.

I couldn't help but laugh with her. "Concussion bullshit. I doubt you're doing much reading right now."

She hummed. "You're right. I don't know how I'm ever going to leave here. Mason and I visit the beach almost every day, and I'm in love. Once we get married in August, how will I ever want to leave?"

"I'm sure Luke will convince you with a honeymoon. Do you know where you're going yet?"

"No." She laughed again. "He's keeping it a secret. I think he's enjoying me trying to get it out of him."

"I'm sure."

"Are you okay, hun? You sound kind of down," she asked, concerned.

"I'm waiting to hear from Holden. It's hard." I sighed, tears building.

"I know it is, but eventually he'll be home and with you."

"I guess you sort of know what I'm going through."

"Sort of. I mean, I couldn't always talk to Luke whenever I wanted to, but I didn't have worry for his safety either. It will make it all the more special when Holden finally gets home."

I let out a deep sigh. "I feel like I just got him back,

and at any moment, he could be taken from me. How is that fair? I can't lose him again."

"It's not fair, but you know life's not fair. If it were, Holden never would have left you. Sometimes we have to go through hell to get our happily ever afters." Truer words had never been spoken.

"You'd know that better than anyone after what your ex put you through." I shook my head. There were so many times I'd wanted to call the police on that asshole, but I knew that if I ever did, he'd make her life even more miserable.

One night, Alex had confided in me that she thought Luke had paid off Decker, her ex. One day, he just stopped being such a prick to her and seemed to try to be a better father to Mason. When I asked if she'd questioned Luke, she only shook her head.

"If all our lives were always easy, then we'd never know how good we had it when it was. Does that make sense?"

"It makes perfect sense. I just worry. Sometimes the tone in Holden's letters and when we Skype—"

"I can't imagine," she interrupted as if she knew how hard it was for me to think about it. "It has to be hard for him to be over there. For all of them, and the things they see. He'll probably have some form of post-traumatic stress when he's done."

"I think he already does. Sometimes his eyes look so

haunted. It scares me. I've tried to get him to talk to me, but he refuses."

"Probably because he doesn't want you to worry."

"Too late," I laughed with a bite to it. "I already do. If I would have known where he was this whole time, all of my hair would be gray."

"Before you know it, he'll be home. You just wait and see." I could hear the smile in her voice.

"What's the best part of finally being able to be in the same place as Luke?" I was curious, but I also wanted to stop talking about my problems.

"Oh, that's easy. The best part is getting to wake up and fall asleep with Luke every day. I made him promise me to always wake me up no matter the time, and he does. Even if it's just to say goodnight. It's priceless, and I know you'll have that one day too."

"I certainly hope so. Thank you for calling me and getting my mind off *everything*. Atticus sleeps like twenty hours a day."

"Do you want me to come back? I can if you need me. I hate thinking of you there all alone with nothing to do. I'm sure Josh would be happy to come visit you. He said your car was totaled, so you're going to need to get a new one. Have Josh take you."

"You're right. It would probably make Holden happy when I talk to him, and eventually, I'm going to want to go somewhere."

"Hey, Prue, do it for you. You can't do everything for Holden, you know?" She sounded too serious.

"I know," I answered her quietly. "Thank you for calling and checking up on me. You know you don't have to. There are worse things out there than being bored."

"If you ever need to talk, I'm here for you. You know that, right?" she asked softly.

"I know. You don't need to be worried about me, Alex. Some days are still hard, but I knew for a long time my dad wasn't going to be around for forever. He fought his best fight, and I'll always miss him, but I know he's in a better place. He's not in any pain anymore, and that's all I can ask for."

"I still miss my dad, and he's been gone for more than ten years," she said quietly.

Alex rarely spoke about her father, but when she did, I could hear how much she missed him. We both had grown up without our mothers in our lives, so our fathers had been everything to us. Alex's mom was a deadbeat who had never been around, and mine had died before I turned two.

"I'll call Josh and see if he'll take me to go look at cars. Do you care if I steal him away from you?"

"Luke might care. I think he's now more Luke's friend than he is mine. I swear Luke stealing all of my friends. Maybe you can come to Hawaii with Josh for the wedding."

"Alex," I warned.

"As friends. I would never suggest…" she stammered.

"No, I know. I want to come to your wedding, but I'm not sure about flying there. I've never been on a plane before."

"Well," she laughed, "you don't really have any other option. I'll understand if you can't make it though, so don't worry about hurting my feelings."

"Thanks, Alex." I smiled. Alex was the best kind of friend I could ask for. "I'm going to try to make it."

Do Dee Do Blup Blup Blup Do Dee Do Blup Blup Blup

"Shit, Alex, I've got to go. That's Holden." I ran into the kitchen where my laptop was sitting.

"Tell him I said hi. I'll talk to you later. Bye."

"Bye." I got off the phone with a little more pep in my step.

18

"HELLO," I ANSWERED A LITTLE OUT OF BREATH FROM my race to my laptop.

"Prue, are you alright?" Holden questioned, brows furrowed with worry.

"I'm perfect now." I smiled so big I thought my cheeks might split in two.

"Yes, you are." He grinned back at me. "I missed seeing your beautiful face these past few days."

A burst of laughter escaped. "Now I know you're shitting me. I've looked in the mirror."

"Scrapes and bruises and all, you're still beautiful."

"Thank you." I blushed, unused to the compliment. "How have you been? I don't mean to be rude, but you look a little tired."

There was no hiding the dark circles that marred Holden's handsome face.

"I was worried about you," he answered in a clipped tone, his mouth in a firm line.

"Why? Alex told you I'd be fine."

I knew she had because I'd read the email she'd sent to him from my account.

"She's all the way in Hawaii. How was she to know if you were really okay or not?"

"Because after I told her to contact you, she asked to talk to my nurse to make sure I wasn't trying to make it sound better than what it was. I'm fine."

Holden cracked a grin. "Because you would totally make it sound not as serious as it was so she wouldn't worry and in turn make me worry."

"I hate how well you know me sometimes." I pouted but didn't mean it.

"No, you don't." He laughed for a moment and then sobered quicker than I could blink. "Don't lie to me. How are you really?"

"Bored out of my fucking mind." Atticus jumped down from the couch and came into the kitchen to drink some water. "Oh," I exclaimed, "you haven't seen Atticus yet. Let me grab him."

I ran to the mudroom where the dog bowls were set up and scooped Atticus up into my arms. Snuggling him to my chest, I buried my nose deep into his fluffy fur.

"Here he is," I sang as I sat down on the barstool, pushing Atticus' face toward the camera.

Holden's face broke into an ear-splitting grin. "He's cute."

"I told you, and he's so soft. I just want to cuddle him all day long. Luckily, he lets me. He might be a little spoiled though." Or a lot.

I reached into the pantry and got him a rawhide bone to chew on before I set him down to play. I didn't need him to find something he shouldn't while I was on with Holden. The little fuzzball had ruined more than a few pairs of shoes because I hadn't watched him closely enough.

"I'm sorry you've been so bored, but it will be over before you know it. Then you can watch TV or movies or read. I guess I shouldn't be expecting too many emails from you until you're healed."

"I can send short ones. I'm the one who should be sorry. I shouldn't complain about being bored. Your enlistment will be over before we know it, and then you'll be here with Atticus and me. He can't wait to meet you."

"Is he the only one excited to see me?" He had a knowing smile on his face.

"I'm beyond excited to see you. You should have seen me run to the computer to answer your call." I laughed.

"You're probably not supposed to be running," he scolded.

I couldn't help but scoff. "It was all of like twenty feet from the living room to the kitchen. I'll be fine."

"Don't risk your health, Prue. It would kill me if something happened to you. When I read that email…" He shook his head. The happiness from earlier gone. "I couldn't breathe. What would my life be without you in it? There would be no point," he said the last so quietly I almost didn't hear him.

"Holden Montgomery, don't you dare say that. Is that what you want if something happens to you? Do you want me to not go on?" I asked, furious.

"Prue," he sighed, "they were only words. It's impossible for me to express how I was feeling when I read that email. I'm not going to lie to you though. You *are* what's keeping me going."

"It's not much longer. In a few months, you'll be home. I wish…"

"What?" He tilted his head, curious.

"That when you were here, we were where we are now. I wish I would have talked to you more."

"While it would have been nice, I understood. I'm just thankful you're talking to me now and giving me a chance. I know I don't deserve it after I left you with no word."

Rolling my eyes, I laughed. "You knew I'd eventually give in, didn't you?"

He looked down, swallowing hard. "In all honesty, no, I didn't know. I hoped with everything I had though."

"Oh Holden," I smiled dreamily at the screen, "even though you look different, I still see my old Holden in there. The one I fell in love with."

"What if you can't love who I am now?" he asked, looking away.

"Are you that much different? Deep down?" I didn't care who he was now, I'd still love him.

He shrugged but looked thoughtful. "In some ways, I'm still the same, and in others, it's as if I'm a completely different person. This place changes you. Seeing what I've seen and doing what I've had to do." Holden closed his eyes, pain etched across every inch of his handsome face.

"You probably have PTS. Anyone who's been over there probably has it. Have you thought about seeing a therapist when you get back?"

"I have no doubt that I have some form of PTS, but I don't know if any therapist can fix me. I've heard so many stories where all they do is drug you up, making you a zombie. I don't want that." His lips turned down. "I know it will be hard to acclimate to the real world. During my brief visits back, the…" He closed his eyes. "Please don't give up on me."

"I won't. I promise you, Holden. I only now got you back. No one and nothing are going to take you away from me," I vowed.

Glassy eyes stared back at me. A smile tugged at his lips.

"Are you okay? I wish you'd talk to me." I sighed, my shoulders slumping.

Talking to Holden had so many ups and downs. There didn't seem to be a safe subject that didn't send his emotions swinging one way or the other. Not that I minded when I said something that made him happy, but it worried me when he was upset and then went out there to do whatever he did.

Would he ever tell me?

"I've been meaning to bring something up before our next mission. I changed my emergency contact information. I put you down, so if anything happens to me…"

"Stop right there. Nothing is going to happen to you. You're going to go wherever it is that you go and be safe and when your tour is up, you're coming home to me. Do you hear me?"

Holden smiled at me sadly. His eyes held knowledge that I wasn't sure he'd ever get around to telling me. "No amount of you bossing me around is going to protect me. I promise you, I do everything in my power to be safe."

"I hope so. I was talking to Alex before you called. She was checking up on me." I shook my head in exasperation while Holden grinned.

"I'm glad someone else can check on you when I can't."

"My car was totaled from the wreck, and I don't have any money saved up yet." I laughed. "I don't even have a job."

His brows pulled together. "What are you talking about? There should be plenty of money in the account. If not, call the lawyer we met with, and he'll put more in."

"Holden, it feels wrong spending your money. I wanted…"

A growl flew out of his mouth, and I could have sworn I felt how pissed-off he was through the computer screen. "Are we married?"

"Yes," I stammered from the venom in his voice.

"Then don't…just don't. That money is as much yours as it is mine," he ground out.

"So, I can buy a bunch of Rolls Royce's and Maserati's if I want?"

"If you want, but I know you, Prue. You'd never drive any of them. I do want you to buy something new and big so that if some asshole hits you again, you'll be safe."

"So, a tank?" I asked with sarcasm.

"Not a tank, smartass. But you need an SUV or a truck of some sort that's four-by-four. It will be sturdy in a wreck and get you around in the snow safely."

"Well, you're bossy today. Do you have any suggestions? Because I've had the same car since I turned sixteen."

He shook his head. "I can't believe you were still driving that piece of shit car. You should have already bought a new one."

"There was no sense in wasting money when my car was fine to drive."

"You might not have a concussion right now if you had been driving something safer." He frowned.

I hated trying to read him through a screen. Sometimes it lagged, making it hard to see his facial expressions and reactions and this was one of those times.

"It was so scary, Holden," I choked out, tears building at the memory.

"You can talk to me about it," he tried to persuade me. It upset me that he wanted me to talk to him since I could never get him to talk to me, but maybe if I talked, he would too, eventually.

"All of a sudden it started pouring when I was on my way home. The streets were flooded, and water was splashing up on my windshield. My wipers couldn't keep up, and there was no place to pull over to. Then a truck coming from the other direction lost control, and that was it. I was hit. Glass broke, and the next thing I knew, an EMT was talking to me. I woke up in the hospital without my phone. Luckily, I remembered Alex's phone number and called her from the hospital. The rest you know."

Holden held his hand to the screen as if he could somehow touch me, and I put mine to his. "I wish I were there so I could hold you. To have you in my arms would be a dream come true."

"I want that too," I croaked out. My nose tingled as emotion built up in my throat.

He looked off into the distance for a moment, and when he refocused on me, sadness filled his chocolatey brown eyes.

"You have to go," I stated as tears started to make their way down my cheeks.

"Yeah, I have to go. I wish I could talk to you all night."

"Me too."

"I love you, Prue. Whenever times are tough, always remember I love you, and I'm coming home to you. Tonight, go look up at the stars and know I'm looking up there with you."

"I love you too, and don't you forget it."

"There's no way in hell that I'd ever forget you telling me you love me. It's what gets me through the days. I'll call you back when I can. Goodbye, Prue."

"Okay. Bye, Holden." I nodded and tried to smile. I was pretty sure I was unsuccessful, but he let it go before disconnecting.

I sank to the floor and laid my head on my knees where I cried until there were no more tears to cry.

19

HOLDEN

To: nurseprue@gmail.com

From: holdenmontgomery@mail.mil

Subject: Talk to You Soon

Date: June 22, 2018 4:59 am

Prue,

I wish I could have called you before we had to head out, but I didn't have time, and you would have been asleep. So, when you get this message, don't worry about me. Go to your doctor's appointment today and get the all clear from your concussion. After that, I want you to get yourself a new car. Let me rephrase that. I want you to get yourself a new SUV that can kick the asses of all the other cars on the road.

I'll call as soon as I can. Until then, know that I'm thinking of you, and I love you.

Love Always,
Holden

I couldn't hear anything but a loud ringing in my ears. I tried to gauge my surroundings, but it was difficult to focus as I struggled to stay conscious. I knew I was hurt. Badly. But I fought against the pull of my consciousness trying to determine if I was still in danger or if anyone in my squad was hurt. The only thing in my periphery was rubble and the Humvee I'd been in when the IED went off. It was almost unrecognizable as it rested on its side engulfed in flames, its frame twisted and mangled.

Someone shook my shoulder, and my eyes fluttered open. It was Rodriguez. He knelt down beside me, and it looked as if he was shouting to get my attention, but no sound was coming out. Worry was etched into the planes of his solemn face. One side of his body was caked in dirt mixed with blood.

My eyes started to droop once more. I was starting to slip away when his voice filtered through. "Montgomery, you've got to stay awake."

"No man, just give me a few minutes to rest, and I'll be as good as new. How are the rest of the guys?" I hadn't been able to get a visual on any of them.

"Samuelson is over with Rico and Tedesco. I don't know how badly they're hurt, but I've called it in. It shouldn't be long until we get you guys out of here."

"I'll be fine. My head just feels a little wonky." Sounds were distorted, and it was difficult to understand what Rodriguez was saying, but I managed. "I probably have a concussion, but I'll be all right, man. Don't worry about me. Me and Prue with our matching concussions." I smiled, my eyes falling closed.

He looked troubled and unsure. "Stay with me, man. Think about your wife and how badly you want to see her."

I wanted to see her so badly. To feel her in my arms and never let her go.

I blinked, and Rodriguez was gone. Everything was gone. I could only see smoke as it became thicker with each passing second. It invaded all my senses. My skin burned, and I choked on the smoke, but I couldn't move. All I could do was cough as my body remained frozen. I was being pulled deeper and deeper into myself, unable to stop from slipping away.

Where had Rodriguez gone?

My last thought was of Prue. Her beautiful face flashed before my eyes as I drifted away.

20

SITTING OUTSIDE ON THE BACK DECK, I SIPPED MY coffee as I watched Atticus chase after a squirrel. It was early. Too early if you asked me, but I hadn't been able to sleep. I'd tried watching a movie last night, which explained my current state of sleep deprivation. When I did fall asleep, I dreamt of Holden, but not the good kind of dream where I woke up rubbing myself against the mattress or with my fingers inside my panties. Instead, I kept dreaming he would be standing in front of me smiling, and then all of a sudden, he'd get a tormented look on his face before he started to fade away until there was nothing left of him.

Finally, I decided to get up and make another pot of coffee. I had a feeling it was going to be a long day. I needed to go to the DMV to pay the taxes on my new car and get plates for it. I was a little nervous about going out by myself. So far, since I'd been home, Alex's friend Josh had driven me, but now that I had a car to drive, I needed to get back in the saddle. I couldn't ask Josh to drive me around forever.

I made it through the DMV with only about a thousand yawns as I waited. I never wanted to go back again. Normally, I would have read on my phone, but I hadn't gotten the all clear yet from my doctor. I probably shouldn't have been driving either, but I wasn't going to call and ask Josh. Surely there had to be some way to make the DMV a more pleasant place to wait. Maybe have dancers to watch. Anything would be better than a bunch of pissed-off people waiting their turn.

As I pulled up to the front of the house, my phone rang with an unknown number. Normally, I wouldn't answer, thinking it was a telemarketer, but something told me I needed to answer the phone. Hitting the button to take the call, I answered. "Hello?"

"Is this Mrs. Montgomery?" an unknown male voice asked.

"This is she," I replied as I parked in the garage.

"Ma'am, I'm Sergeant Bishop, I regret to inform you that your husband has been seriously injured. He's being taken to Germany where he'll receive surgery for his injuries and continue to stay there until he can be moved stateside."

NO! No. No. No. NO!

Holden couldn't be hurt. I refused to believe it. I didn't want to believe that he could be taken from me before we were really even an us.

"Mrs. Montgomery, are you still there?" he asked, concerned.

"Yes, I'm still here," I sobbed out. "Is my husband going to be okay?"

"There's no way for me to answer that right now. I can keep you informed as I find out more information. Since it may be some time before Sergeant Montgomery is brought back to the states, you have the right to come to Germany to be with him."

"I want to be with him. What do I need to do?" I asked, stumbling out of my car and into the house so I could take notes.

Everything was a blur after I got off the phone. I booked my flights, packed, and headed to the airport. Once I was on my way, I called Alex to let her know what was going on and Josh to look after Atticus. After that, I briefly remembered going from one airport to the next. All my life I'd been afraid to fly, but my need to be by Holden's side overrode everything in me. The next thing I knew, I was being greeted by a nurse at the front desk of the hospital.

"Ma'am," I sagged with relief that she spoke English. "I regret to inform you that Sergeant Montgomery has requested to have no visitors." The nurse had the decency to look away.

"What?" I whisper-yelled. "I've been flying and trying to get here for two days, and now you're saying I can't see my husband?" My legs felt unsteady as everything caught up; I leaned against the wall.

"No, ma'am, you could see him, but he doesn't…he doesn't want *any* visitors," she tried to say as delicately as possible.

"Could you please tell him that I'm here and want to see him?" I asked, slumping into the wall.

"Of course, but I can't promise you that he'll change his mind."

"Well, you tell him that I'm not going anywhere until I see him. I didn't fly all this way to get turned around at the door. I've never flown a day in my life, but I got myself on a plane. For him."

"I understand, and I'm sorry. Sergeant Montgomery was in surgery when you were called. I'll relay your message."

"You do that," I snapped, instantly feeling guilty. It wasn't anyone else's fault that Holden didn't want to see me. If he wasn't hurt, I would rip him a new asshole for taking at least ten years off my life and then refusing to see me.

I sat in the nearest chair, determined to not break down, but the moment the nurse stepped in front of me and I saw the look on her face, I crumbled. Sobs wracked my body. I pulled my knees to my chest with my forehead against them. Why didn't he want to see me? Did Holden not remember me? Did he have amnesia, and that's why he didn't want to see me?

My head popped up to talk to the nurse, but she was already gone. I didn't blame her. It wasn't enjoyable to watch someone break down, and I was sure she had to see it more often than not. I had no idea how long I cried before any rational thought came to me. I ran to the desk where I'd found the nurse and started peppering her with questions. "Can you give me updates? Does my husband have amnesia? Is that why he doesn't want to see me? Because he can't remember who I am? If that's the case, maybe if he sees me, he'll remember?"

"I'm sorry, but his mental faculties seem to be intact. Right now, he's depressed, and he wishes to be left alone."

"If I can't see him, can you tell me what happened? What his injuries are if it isn't amnesia?"

"I can assure you that your husband doesn't have amnesia. It's very common that our patients request no visitors once they wake up. Give him some time, and I'm sure he'll come around. Right now, though, he's in a very bad place."

"But I could help him if he's in a bad place. I've

known Holden since high school, and I know I could help him if he'd only let me."

"I'm sure that's the case, but right now, we have to abide by his wishes. I'm sorry. I hate to be the bearer of bad news, but if it were you, I'm sure you'd want us to do as you ask."

"Yes, of course. I understand you're doing your job. What I don't understand is why my husband doesn't want to see me. All we've talked about for the last few months is that we can't wait to see each other, and now that we can, he's refusing to see me," I cried, tears streaming down my cheeks as reality set in.

My husband, the love of my life, didn't want to see me.

"Give him time, honey."

I didn't want to give him time. I'd nearly lost my mind more than once as each plane took off and landed, all with the thought that I might lose Holden. I had no idea how injured he was. How could he be so cruel?

21

PRUE

FOR THE PAST FEW DAYS, MY HOME WAS THE WAITING room of the hospital in Germany. Holden still refused to see me, but I was not going to give up. There was no way in hell I was leaving, even if I had to stay in the waiting room the entire time.

The nurses had taken pity on me. They'd brought me a blanket, pillow, and scrubs to change into. Every day, they'd let Holden know I was still there, and every day he told them he didn't want to see me. He'd asked that they didn't relay any information on him. As they looked at me with pity in their eyes, I stopped asking. With Holden refusing to see me, all I had time to do was think. Think about what had happened and how he was injured. I knew he'd had surgery but not why.

My imagination had run away from me thinking the worst things possible. I knew it wasn't good, otherwise Holden would have been taken back to the states. My thoughts ranged from him being only a torso to his entire body being burned. Being burned made sense as to why Holden didn't want me to see him. Each day I waited, the angrier I got. I had a feeling that was Holden's intent. He wanted me to get pissed-off and leave.

But it didn't matter to me if he was burned all over his body. Yes, Holden was beyond handsome, but I didn't fall in love with his looks. I fell in love with the man he was, and it was going to take a lot more than him pushing me away to make me stop loving him. If I hadn't stopped when he left me, I sure as hell wasn't going to stop now.

The nurses urged me to leave if only for a few minutes. To get out and take a walk, have a real meal, or a shower, but I couldn't leave. What if Holden changed his mind and wanted to see me while I was gone?

After a week, with a crick in my neck, I was over giving Holden his space. I needed to see him. I needed to see him with my own eyes to know that he was okay. After that, I could leave.

I stopped by the vending machine to grab a bag of chips when I heard Holden's name. I inched closer trying to hear a little better, but when I turned the corner they were gone. My gaze flicked up and down the hall. No one was around, and I took the opportunity to venture further into the hospital. A nurse passed by, and I held my breath, but she didn't stop me. No one stopped me as I slowly took in my surroundings and inched down the hallway. At each door, I read the name and continued on until I was standing in front of a room marked H. Montgomery. With shaky hands, I looked both ways, making sure the coast was clear before I turned the knob and slipped inside.

My breath caught as I took in the man in front of me. His face was bruised and swollen, but underneath it all, I could see my Holden. From what little I could tell, he wasn't burned all over his body, so why had he not wanted me to see him?

My eyes scanned every inch of his body, slowly I started to relax seeing his chest as it rose and fell. He wasn't hooked up to any machines which was a good sign. One hand was bandaged, but not in a cast. An IV stuck out of his other hand. I continued to take him in and stopped dead when his left leg that rested on a pillow stopped halfway down from his knee.

Tears filled my eyes as my hand went to my mouth. This was why he didn't want me to see him. Did he think I wouldn't want him any longer? Did he think I'd be repulsed?

"I told them not to let you in," he growled out. I was unsure how he knew I was in the room. He hadn't opened his eyes and continued to keep them closed.

"Holden," I gasped out and ran to the side of the bed where I grabbed the hand with the IV.

"You need to leave, Prue, before I call for security to escort you out."

"You'd really do that?" My chin trembled.

"I asked to be left alone. How'd you get back here anyway?" He opened his eyes only to turn and look away.

"I snuck in. It wasn't my intention." I shook my head. Who cared? "I was grabbing a bite to eat," I held up the chip bag, "when I heard your name." I shrugged. "When I noticed there was no one around, I started to look for you."

"Well, you found me and now you can un-find me. Go back to your house and live your life."

"My life is with you. When you get better, you're coming home. I…"

"I'm never going to get better, Prue," he interrupted. "This is me now."

"Of course, you're going to get better. You'll heal. I…know this is a big change, but you're strong, Holden. You can get through anything. We can get through this."

He turned to me, his eyes cold as he spit his words at me. "I don't want to get through it, and I sure as hell don't want you to get through *this*. I never wanted you to see me like *this*."

"Holden, don't. I love you and nothing can change that."

His throat bobbed with emotion as his eyes filled with pain. "Go home, Prue. Start to live your life. When the two years are up, you'll receive the paperwork to dissolve our marriage. Don't worry, you'll be taken care of."

"I don't want your fucking money, Holden. I only want you. You can't do this to us," I sobbed out the last few words unable to hold back my devastation.

"It's already been done to us. Look at me, Prue." He slammed his hands down on the bed. "I'm never going to be whole again. Don't you understand that?"

"Yes, I do understand and I. Don't. Care. You're alive, and that's all that matters."

"Please, just go home, Prue. Don't sit there and look at me with your sad eyes begging me."

"You really want me to go home?"

A tear slipped off my chin and dripped onto his hand. Holden's gaze followed, and for a moment, I thought he was going to change his mind. Then his face went blank, and I knew I'd lost him.

"I don't want you anymore," he said with his jaw set.

Standing, I stumbled to the door and looked back one last time.

"Goodbye, Holden."

22

HOLDEN

Turning toward the wall, I couldn't watch Prue walk out the door, even if I had been the one who pushed her away. I tried to get accustomed to the boulder that sat on my chest. Each word I spoke to Prue made it heavier and heavier until it became almost impossible to breathe. When I saw the tears in her eyes, I knew that I had made the right choice in making her go.

Prue didn't deserve to have to take care of me, to watch me struggle and learn how to live life again with part of my leg missing. She'd taken care of her father for so long, and I wanted her to be free to do whatever she wanted. Not to be burdened by me and the life she'd lead if she stayed.

For the past few months, I had been searching within myself to figure out what I wanted to do once I

149

got home. A home I had now given up for a second time. I had thought about becoming a cop in Fairlane or around the area, but now I had no idea what I wanted to do. Being a cop was out of the question, and so was being with Prue. I knew I could always go to college and become an architect like I'd wanted to do back in high school, but I couldn't imagine spending the next four years sitting in a classroom.

I was lost in more ways than one, and I had no idea if I'd ever find myself.

I had to keep telling myself that I had done the right thing sending Prue away, but as each day passed, the hole in my chest grew larger and the boulder became heavier. I started to second guess myself and my choices. If I hadn't been in the hospital, I would have been in a bar drinking until I was blackout drunk. Instead, all I could do was stare at the walls and avoid the narrowed eyes from the nurses.

I had nothing to do but think about my situation.

Before, I thought being separated from Prue was bad, but it was nothing like winning her back only to send her away. The thought of never seeing her smiling face or her beautiful green eyes light up when she looked at me, killed me inside.

Closing my eyes, I prayed that I would wake up from this nightmare.

Instead, I was greeted each and every day by the nightmare that had become my life.

I'd lost a part of me.

My leg.

And Prue.

23

I CRIED THE ENTIRE WAY HOME. TWO DAYS OF GUT-wrenching sobs while strangers stared at me, but I didn't care. My life was over. When I got home, I headed straight to bed where I stayed for the rest of the night. The next day, I called Alex, needing a friend and someone to tell me what to do.

"Prue?" she answered.

Alex had once again saved me. She didn't know the details because I hadn't known much, only that Holden had been injured and was being flown to a hospital in Germany. She called Josh, who had come by and picked up Atticus while I was gone.

"Yeah, it's me." My voice was nearly gone from all the crying I'd done the past week.

"How bad is it?"

"It's over," I cried out.

"What do you mean, it's over?" she asked, confused.

"Me and Holden. Our marriage. He sent me away," I barely choked out.

"Wha…what? That doesn't make sense. He worked so hard to get you back. Tell me everything," she demanded softly.

I told her everything from the time I'd gotten to the hospital until the moment I left Germany.

"Oh, honey. I'm so sorry. I don't know what to tell you. I think Holden needs more time to come to terms with what happened to him. It can't be easy to wake up with half your leg missing."

"I know, but I don't know how to convince him that I don't care about his leg. How do I get him to come home when this isn't really even his home? I just assumed he would be moving to Fairlane when he finally got out. He had asked if he could visit, but now I don't know."

"From everything that you've told me, I think he was planning on staying. Does he have a house somewhere else for him to go to when he gets stateside?"

"Not that I know of. I mean, he has the money to do whatever he wants. He could have bought three houses since I left."

"I seriously doubt it. You've got to get him to Fairlane," she said, determined.

"How am I going to do that? He's an adult. I can't make arrangements for him and expect for them to be followed."

"Does he have any way to communicate? A computer or phone?"

Good question. I knew absolutely nothing.

"I should have stayed in Germany, but after what he said, I was too upset to think clearly. I could have ambushed him when he was leaving."

Alex laughed. "I don't think that would have worked the way you're thinking. Maybe you can call and see where he'll be sent once he's back. He'll have to go through therapy and learn to walk again. He won't go straight home wherever that is."

"So, you're saying to stake my claim there and make him come back to Fairlane?"

"That's exactly what I'm saying. If it was the other way around, he would throw you over his shoulder and manhandle you into doing what he wanted. Well, I don't know that Holden would do that since I don't really know him."

"Luke wouldn't do that," I told her knowingly.

"No, he wouldn't," she laughed. "I've read too many romance novels."

"You can never read too many romance novels." I leaned my head back and let out a frustrated breath.

"God, I don't know what to do. Tell me about Hawaii. I need to hear something good."

"Are you sure? Because," she sighed, dreamily, "it's perfect here. If I could, I'd live here. You know I love the beach."

"I do. I know if you could have, you would've moved with your friend, Taylor to Florida." I laughed for the first time in days.

"There was no way Decker would have ever let me move, but you're right, I would have."

"Tell me what it's like there." I needed to get my mind off Holden.

"It's beautiful. Absolutely gorgeous. The water is so pretty, and everything is so green. We've ventured to a few waterfalls. The best word to describe it is paradise. Mason and I spend half the day at the beach and the other half exploring."

"Is Luke sad that he's missing out on a lot of it?"

"A little bit, but he understands that the beach can't entertain Mason for the entire time he's here. I would be perfectly fine spending all my time there though." She laughed. "I wish you could come to the wedding, but I understand why you can't."

"I hate that I'll probably have to miss it now that I've gotten over my fear of flying, but…"

"Don't worry about it. If you need me to come

home, I can. I feel bad that I'm here in paradise, and you're going through hell."

"Do you think Holden will change his mind?" I asked, afraid to hear her answer, but also hoping she would put my fears at ease.

"I truly think he will. He just needs time. What would you do if you lost a limb? He's looking out for you. He knows how much you loved your dad and how hard it was to take care of him. He doesn't want to do the same thing to you."

"I have loved Holden since I was fifteen years old. For years, I thought I'd never see him again, and then he shows up out of the blue. I tried so hard to not let him in, afraid that he'd hurt me, and what happened?" I closed my eyes as a single tear slipped down my cheek.

"Honey, he was already in, you were just denying it to yourself. You never stood a chance."

"But what if he's serious and never wants anything to do with me again?"

"From what you've told me, I don't think that's the case. He loves you, and I'm sure he always has," she tried to reassure me.

"It would be so much easier if he had a phone or a computer so I could talk to him. I just wish I could talk to him, just once."

"I know, sweetie. Get him a phone or computer

when he gets back. That way you can communicate with him. It might make it easier for him to talk to you if he knows that you can't see him."

"Thank you, Alex. I feel like my brain is mush from all the crying I've done this week."

She made a sad noise on the other end of the line. "If you ever need to talk, call me day or night. I'm here for you."

"I know you are. I don't know what I'd do without you. You're a Godsend."

"I'm happy I could help. Do you feel any better?"

"Sort of, but not really." I laughed. "I'm going to call Josh so I can pick up Atticus. I miss him and hopefully, his cuteness will make me forget about Holden for a few minutes."

"You'll be lucky if Josh gives him back. The couple of times I've talked to him, he talked all baby talk to Atticus. I think he loves the mutt."

"Atticus is easy to love. He's so damn cute and cuddly, but I'm not letting Josh have him." I laughed and grabbed up my keys. Josh wasn't keeping him for another minute.

"I have to agree from the pictures you've sent and posted online. Plus, what Josh has sent." She giggled madly. "I'm just kidding. He hasn't sent any pictures, but he did seriously talk all gaga at him."

"Go enjoy paradise, and I'll talk to you later. Thank you again for everything."

"It doesn't feel like enough, but I'm happy I could help even if it's just a little bit. Keep me updated."

"Will do. Bye, Alex."

"Bye, Prue." She disconnected.

On a mission, I headed out to get my dog and the technology that would hopefully make Holden talk to me and eventually come back to me again.

24

FOR THE PAST TWO DAYS, I'D BEEN HOLED UP IN A rental house in San Diego waiting for Holden to finally get stateside. Now that he was finally here, I was nervous about whether or not he'd refuse to see me.

"Mrs. Montgomery, I'll take the computer and phone, but I can't promise you anything else. Sergeant Montgomery has expressed explicitly he wants no visitors. It will be up to him if he chooses to contact you."

"I understand. Thank you for helping me out. I don't know any other way to get him to talk to me," I confessed, looking down at the floor.

"It happens more than you realize. These warriors have their pride, and after being injured, they push the ones they love away. It takes a strong spouse to get their mate through the tough times."

"I'm trying," I croaked out. "I only saw him once, a

month ago. I snuck into his room. He refused to see me and then…"

"Stay strong." The nurse patted me on the shoulder. "I'll make sure he gets the items, and that he knows they're from you. Are you going to stay in the area or are you going back home?"

"For now, I'm going to stay here. I'm hoping Holden won't take long to at least contact me. If he changes his mind, I want to be able to get to him as fast as I can," I explained.

Giving me a small smile, she turned to set down the box I'd brought for Holden. I'd brought his favorite movie, music, a new phone, and computer, along with some new clothes.

"Good luck, dear. I'll keep you in my prayers. You've got your work cut out for you."

I nodded because I knew it wouldn't be easy, but if I didn't try, I'd always wonder and regret not trying to convince him that we could have a life together. A life I wanted desperately no matter the damage.

"Thank you, Rebecca for all your help." I wanted to hug her for being so nice and seeming to want to help me. I could use all the help I could get.

"You're welcome. I'm sure I'll see you soon."

Every few days, I called or went by the hospital, and every time, I received the same news: Holden still didn't want to see me. Rebecca informed me Holden hadn't opened the computer or turned on his phone. He spent most of his days staring at the ceiling, saying nothing.

Every day I wrote Holden an email. Sometimes I wrote him multiple times a day saying little things I thought he'd like to hear or that would move him to talk to me. I left voicemails in case he turned on his phone first. I was desperate for anything to work. But as days turned to weeks, I slowly started to lose hope. I'd rented a house close to the beach. Atticus and I spent most of our time walking along the water line or sitting outside. It was as if he could feel my pain and wanted to stay close. As far as I was concerned, he was the best dog anyone could ask for.

Then one day as I was leaving the hospital, I saw one of the vets with a service dog. When I got home that night, I researched everything I could, and the next day I contacted a local program that trained dogs for veterans. I was hoping they would take Atticus into their program and train him for Holden. If I thought Holden had PTS before the accident, I was sure he had it now, and he could use all the help he could get. Atticus was the sweetest dog, and I knew he could help if Holden gave him a chance. The only problem was, it would take at least a year or two to train Atticus. I knew it wouldn't take Holden that long to be released out into the world, and I wanted to be ready for him whenever that was.

I put in an application for Holden and enrolled Atticus into training. Even if he couldn't be totally trained, I wanted him to be able to help as much as possible. Luckily, we could afford a dog unlike most of the vets who needed them. When I found out how many relied on grants to get the dogs they needed, I decided to donate money to help out a few others who needed one. It was the right thing to do, and Holden had plenty of money.

We were sitting outside on the deck, Atticus chewing on a rawhide while I watched children run in and out of the surf, when my phone rang. I reached over to answer without looking. Alex was the only person who called me, and it had been a few days since we'd last talked. When a gruff, pissed-off voice answered from the other end my heart nearly stopped.

"Why do I have an email stating that I've applied for a service animal?" Holden growled out.

"Holden," I gasped, jumping up from my seat. Atticus barked and jumped up as well. His little tail wagged thinking we were going to play.

"Answer me," he snarled.

"I wa-wanted to help," I stammered out. "At first, I was going to try to train Atticus, but the…"

"I don't give a shit what you were going to do. I don't want or need a fucking service dog, Prue. And I don't need you or your help."

"Oh really?" I shot back. "And what do you have planned for when you get out of the hospital? Do you even have a house to stay in?"

"What I do doesn't concern you," he spat.

"Everything you do concerns me, Holden. Just because you want to be an asshole doesn't make that any less true. Do you really want to lose what we have?" My voice broke on the last word. How could he be so cruel to me after everything we'd gone through? More than once, he'd told me I was his life. That I was what got him through the day. What was getting him through it now?

He sighed with annoyance. "We don't have anything. Not anymore. Why can't you understand that? It's a simple concept."

"Because I have loved you since I was fifteen years old. Why can't you understand that?" I asked annoyed.

"You don't want me," he answered softly.

"But I do want you, Holden. I've wanted you for so long, and now when I finally got you, you're trying to slip out of my grasp."

"How can you want half a man?" His voice was broken.

"Even if you were a quarter of a man. A quarter of *you*, I'd still want you. But you're not half a man. You're so much more than you're giving yourself credit for."

"Prue," he scolded.

"No," I interrupted. "I understand you need time to come to terms with losing part of your leg. I can't imagine what you're going through, but I want to be there for you."

"You don't know what you're asking," he choked out.

"I don't think you know what you're asking by trying to make me leave. I should have the right to choose what I want to do with my life. You've already done this once and that didn't work out well for either one of us."

"This is for the best. I'm a mess and don't want you to have to spend the rest of your life taking care of me."

I knew that if I were standing in front of him in that moment, I would have seen tears in his eyes. My chest ached at the thought, and I wanted nothing more than to see him and pull him into my arms.

"Holden," I said softly, "I know it doesn't seem like it right now, but it isn't always going to be this way. In a couple of months, you'll be healed up enough to get fitted for a prosthetic. In the meantime, you can walk with crutches or other devices. Yes, life will be different for you, but I can promise you'll have a good life. We'll have a good life. One with endless possibilities. All you have to do is stop trying to push me away because if you keep pushing, eventually, you'll get your wish."

He was quiet for several long minutes. At one point, I pulled my phone away to see if he'd hung up. "Do you really believe that?" I could have sworn I heard hope in his voice, or it might have been my own hope reflecting back at me.

"I wouldn't have said it if I didn't believe it."

Beep. Beep. Beep.

He hung up.

25

I couldn't take the hope in Prue's voice, so instead, I hung up on her. I knew I shouldn't have called her, but I was so pissed-off and had been staring at her phone number scribbled on a piece of paper since I'd arrived in San Diego. I picked up the phone and spat my venom at her only for Prue's words to slowly start to sink in.

Most of the time I knew that, of course, I could have a life; a good life with part of my leg missing, but it wasn't the life I'd envisioned having with Prue once I got home. From the time I saw her in the parking lot after her father's funeral, I knew I'd do everything within my power to get her back. I knew it wouldn't be easy, and it hadn't been, but I'd finally gotten my girl. For months, I'd fantasized about the first time I would see her again. The first time I would have her in my arms. I was going to ravish her for hours on end until we both couldn't move and then start up again until she was pregnant with my child.

Now I couldn't imagine having her look at me with the sheet not covering me up, let alone letting her see me without clothes. What would she think once she finally saw my leg? Would she leave once she saw how grotesque I was? Those were the thoughts that had run through my mind since I'd woke up and learned they'd had to amputate my leg halfway between my ankle and knee. But after getting off the phone with Prue, I couldn't help but think maybe she wouldn't run when she finally got a good look at my leg.

For the next week, my mind was on a loop of what she'd said. Could she really see me the way she thought she could? Could I let her? Finally, I couldn't wonder anymore. I sent her a text asking her to come visit me the next day. Her response was immediate, and I wondered yet again if I'd made the right choice.

I didn't sleep the night before. My insides twisted in knots as I imagined the horrified look on her face when she saw the new me. Once the sun came up, I didn't have long to wait until Prue peeked around the door of my room. Her eyes were bright, but I could see her apprehension as she took her first step into the room.

"Hi," she said quietly.

My eyes trailed over her slim figure. She'd lost more

weight, and I knew I was to blame. Even being too skinny and with no makeup on, she was still the most beautiful woman in the world to me. Her hair trailed down her back. She wore a baggy t-shirt that I knew had once fit her, short shorts, and flip flops. Every inch of skin was a nice, golden brown.

"Hi," I answered back just as faintly.

"Thanks for asking me to come." She stepped closer with unsure steps. "I wasn't sure if you ever would."

"I wasn't either. I'm still not sure if this is a good idea or not," I confessed.

Standing at the edge of the bed with her eyes locked on mine, she asked, "What would you do if I lost an arm or a leg?"

"You know what I'd do," I answered a little too harshly causing her to step back. "It wouldn't matter to me."

"Yet, you still want to push me away." Her voice conveyed how that broke her heart,

"I don't want this life for you. You could have so much better than me. This is just the beginning. Who knows how fucked I'll be out there in the real world? I can barely function here in a hospital. What's going to happen when I leave?"

"I don't know, but I'll be there with you every step of the way if you'll let me."

"Prue," I shook my head and let out a deep breath, "how many times can I tell you that I don't want that life for you? You spent so long taking care of your dad, and now me?"

"I'm a nurse, Holden, I like taking care of people." I started to interrupt her, but she continued on with narrowed eyes. "I don't get some sick, perverted feeling from it, but I'm not one to run away from taking care of the people I love. Yes, it sucked taking care of my dad day and night in the end, but only because I knew he was going to die. Those were my last moments with him. Now it's so hard to remember him healthy."

Tears slowly trickled down her face as she became lost in the thought of her dad. He had meant everything to her. They were each other's worlds and never fought.

"I hate that that's your final memory of your dad. If I could change it, I would. That's why you should leave and not look back. I don't want you to think of me—"

"You're being ridiculous, you know that?" she interrupted, her mouth set in a pissed-off line. "You do realize you're not dying, right?"

"Some days, it sure feels like it," I murmured.

Prue's face went soft, and she slipped around the side of the bed. Her warm hand wrapped around mine. "I'm going to ask you something, and I want you to be honest. Can you do that?"

"Of course, I can be honest with you." That's all I'd ever been with her.

"Even if you don't want to."

"Yes, I promise to answer you honestly. Just ask your question."

She nodded to herself as if she was preparing herself for what she was going to ask. "Do you love me?"

How could she ask that? I'd always loved her and knew I always would.

"I love you with everything that I am. I don't see what that has to with anything."

A slow smile spread across her gorgeous face. "If you didn't love me, then I would have left. It would have hurt immensely, but I would have walked away."

"And now?" I asked almost inaudibly. I wasn't sure how she heard me.

"And now you're not getting rid of me."

"Wait until you see what you'll have to live with for the rest of your life before you promise you won't leave. I won't blame you if you leave once you see." And I wouldn't. It wasn't pretty and not something anyone would want to see every day of their life.

"I vowed to stick with you through sickness and health."

I laughed bitterly. "You didn't marry me out of love."

Her eyes grew big before narrowing into slits. "Did you seriously just say that, Holden Ford Montgomery? You think I didn't love you? I just told you that I've loved you since I was fifteen years old. I never stopped." She turned away, her face falling, and for a moment I saw how much my words had hurt her.

"You didn't want to get married," I reminded her.

Her head whipped my way. "Yeah, I didn't want to get married for you to then divorce me. At the time, I thought you were marrying *me* out of pity." Her eyes filled with tears once again. "We should have talked before."

I scoffed. "If we would have talked, you wouldn't have married me. You would have stayed pissed at me and then never talked to me again."

"Well, I want to clear this up once and for all, okay? I loved you when we got married. I was sad because I hated that you were marrying me for money and out of pity, and that you didn't love me. Which I now know wasn't true. Yes, I was mad at you, but…" Angry tears streamed down her flushed cheeks. "Damn if you're right in the fact that I probably wouldn't have married you."

"Why don't you come over here?" I patted the right side of the bed. I hated to see her cry, and it seemed like that's all she'd done the past few times I'd seen her. I hated being responsible for her tears.

Prue took in a ragged breath before she quickly moved around the side of the bed and curled up next to me, burying her head into my chest. And fuck if she didn't feel perfect. She still smelled like vanilla after all these years, and it was like coming home. My arms wrapped around her shaking form and held her to me.

"I missed this," she mumbled into my t-shirt.

My lips tipped up. How had I thought I could give her up?

Then a nurse walked in with my pain medicine, and I remembered why I had pushed Prue away. This was my life now. It wasn't love, hugs, and snuggles.

26

PRUE

THE MOMENT THE NURSE WALKED INTO THE ROOM, I felt Holden tense underneath me and knew he was going to try and push me away again. A-fucking-gain.

"Oh, it's so nice to see you with a visitor. Is this your wife?" the nurse asked.

He grunted, not even answering as he took the cup, threw back the meds, and then the water. His hands laid at his sides, no longer around me. I missed their warmth and the way they made me feel hope for the first time in weeks.

Once the nurse left, I sat up to look at him, only to find Holden looking out the window with his mouth turned down, his face tight.

I'd lost him again.

But this time, I wasn't giving up.

I wished he'd realize his life wouldn't be like this forever.

"Hey," I called, placing my hand on his stubbled cheek, "come back."

Endlessly dark brown eyes met mine with a frown. "Prue…"

"No," I stopped him, "don't you dare say it. I'm not going anywhere."

"You're fucking stubborn," he grumbled.

"And so are you. A nurse walks in, and you're ready to give me up?"

"I'm never going to want this life for you. I can't help that."

"And I can't help that I'll always want to be in your life. So, accept that and stop being an ass."

"Easier said than done."

I shifted around so that I was facing him on the bed. "Tell me something. What were your plans once you finally got out in a few months? Don't hold back."

"Why are you asking me that now? It doesn't matter." He scowled and tried to look away, but I turned his face back to me.

"Tell me," I demanded.

"Fine. I was going to come straight to Fairlane. Happy?"

"And then what?" Because I knew there was more.

"You don't want to know." He laughed bitterly.

"Stop that shit. If I didn't want to know, then I wouldn't ask. Now tell me."

"Fine," he growled out. "I planned to not let you out of bed for at least a week, then I was going to take you on a honeymoon to wherever you wanted to go."

"And then?"

"I don't know what you want me to say, Prue. I'm a guy. I was planning lots and lots of sex."

"Okay, let's start with that then. Anywhere I want to go on a honeymoon?"

"That's what I said I was planning," His jaw ticked.

I hummed to myself. "Well, after listening to Alex, I want to go to Hawaii. It sounds perfect. If we left from here, it wouldn't be that long of a flight."

"I said I was…"

"What? You don't want to anymore?" I knew my eyes were big and probably looked as if they might pop out of my head.

"This is what I'm talking about, Prue. You're already disappointed in me."

"Explain to me why the plan has changed."

"Don't be stupid, Prue. You know exactly why." Each word was laced with disappointment.

"Because of your leg?" I questioned. Why did he think he couldn't do anything anymore?

"Yes, because of my fucking leg. It's fucking gone,"

he shouted then ground his teeth together as he looked at me with furious eyes.

"Holden, you are going to walk again," I stated softly. "No, you're not going to jump out of bed tomorrow walking, but it is going to happen. Then you can do whatever you want, including going on our honeymoon and keeping me in bed for a month."

He shook his head before turning to look out the window again. "You make it sound easy."

"I know it isn't going to be easy, but I know you and how strong and persistent you are. Don't let this keep you down. The only way it is going to rule your life is if you let it."

"You're annoying. You know that, right?" He took a deep breath as he looked deep inside me for a long moment. "I know I don't deserve you, but thank you for being here, Prue."

"I wouldn't be anywhere else. Thanks for finally getting your head out of your ass and letting me visit you."

We sat quietly for a few moments looking at each other. I wanted to touch him desperately, but I wasn't sure if he was ready for my touch. I knew it was likely that when I came back tomorrow, he might refuse to see me again, and I'd have to battle him again.

How many times would he try to push me away before he realized I was never letting him go?

I knew I had to steel myself for the inevitable hurt that was sure to invite itself along on this journey with Holden. My heart already ached at seeing how difficult this was on him, and I knew it would only get harder once he had to start therapy and get his prosthetic.

My fingers twitched at my side longing to reach out to him.

"What happened?" he asked quietly, his index finger traced along the top of my hand.

His simple touch made me want to cry, and I knew I needed to get ahold of myself.

I shrugged not wanting to answer him.

"Don't keep to yourself. Tell me what's going on in that pretty head of yours." His quiet words spurred me on.

I took a deep breath and held it as I stared into his soft gaze. I needed to be truthful with him and not hold back. I knew that, but it was so hard when his emotional stability was at risk. Blowing out a deep breath, I hooked my pinky with his index finger.

"I was thinking about how many more times you were probably going to push me away and how much it hurt when you didn't want to see me. I raced as fast as I could to Germany only to be told that I couldn't see you. I don't want to go through that again," I choked out, a tear slipping down my cheek.

"Fuck, Prue." My name sounded as if it got caught

in his throat. Choked and garbled. "Come here." His hands reached around me and pulled me up the bed like I had been earlier. I slipped my arm around his waist and held him as tightly as I could.

"Hey," his hand ran down my hair and back, "I'm not going anywhere."

Loosening my hold, I scooted up and buried my face in his neck, my nose running along the column of his throat as I took in his spicy scent that had somehow managed to stick with him even without his soap and aftershave. "You still smell the same."

He chuckled and held me closer. "What do I smell like?"

"It's going to sound silly, but you smell like home. That was my thought when you showed up in Fairlane. Warmth and spice." I shrugged. "Home."

"It doesn't sound silly," he replied his voice full of emotion.

I tilted my head back to get a good look at him. His eyes were closed, and his face was serene as he twirled a piece of my hair.

"I love you," I whispered.

Holden's eyes opened with fire in them. His hand that had been playing with my hair pulled me closer until our lips were only a breath away. His eyes flicked down to my mouth and back up to catch my gaze before he erased the distance between us and brushed his lips to mine.

Instantly, I was on fire. It had been too long since I'd been with a man and too long since Holden had touched me. "Holden," I groaned out his name. My tongue swept along his full lips, desperate to get inside and taste him. He opened for me, and I dove in. Exploring every inch of his mouth, our tongues dueled and danced. My fingers tried to tangle in the short hairs at his neck, and when they were unsuccessful, my hands wandered along the expanse of his muscled back.

Pulling away, Holden nipped my bottom lip and then proceeded to lick and suck down the column of my neck and then back up to my ear. "Fuck Prue, you taste so damn good."

"So do you," I moaned as his tongue twirled around my earlobe. "You're so much more."

My nails scraped along his scalp as I ground myself against him. Not even thinking about how we were in a hospital room and someone might walk in on us.

"Oh God, I feel like a teenager." I bit down on his shoulder to hide my moan. "I need your mouth."

His lips came back to mine, swallowing my pleasure as I rode out my orgasm on his leg.

My hand slowly snaked down his body, getting acquainted with muscles that weren't there years ago.

My passion reignited with each ridge and ripple I explored. As my hand moved underneath the covers, a firm hand stopped my movement.

"Prue," he warned.

My eyes flew up to see his face tight.

"Let me touch you," I coaxed.

"Not today."

27

PRUE

HOLDEN GROWLED, PULLED MY HANDS AWAY FROM HIS body, and threw his head back against his pillow. It had been a week since he'd let me see him, and so far, he hadn't pushed me away except physically. We've been like two teenagers dry humping in their parents' home except in a hospital room. Well, I was the one humping him, and he let me have my way until I tried to move my touching south of the border. Each and every time, he would growl my name and pull my hands away. I couldn't figure out why, and the one time I tried to ask him, I got the silent treatment, so I let it go for the time being.

I knew he wanted me. I could feel as his hard length poking me through his sweatpants, yet every time I made any attempt to touch him, he pulled away.

"You should probably head out to check on Atticus." He leaned over and kissed my temple as if that would help ease the sting of his rejection.

"In a little bit. I love Atticus, but I only get to spend so much time with you."

Holden made me leave every time someone came in to look him over, and after the first couple of times when he didn't want to do anything but stare out the window afterwards, I learned to leave him to himself.

I couldn't imagine what he was going through, and I knew it was a lot to come to terms with, but it killed me each time he shut down on me. Each time, I feared he'd push me away again, but I still had faith.

"You need to start taking better care of yourself, Prue. You're too skinny. You've lost more weight since the beginning of the year. Grab yourself a big, juicy hamburger or a pizza."

"How about I do that and bring you something back too? You've got to be tired of hospital food."

I knew I needed to eat more and gain back the weight I'd lost, but it was hard when I was constantly worried. His gaze flicked over my face before he looked out the window. Fuck, he was retreating into himself again, and I hated it. I desperately wanted to make him talk to me but knew that wasn't the answer.

"What's wrong?" My fingertip traced along the tattoo that ran along the length of his arm.

Sighing, he blinked and looked back at me with a

raw determination. I knew instantly whatever it was, I wasn't going to like it. "I think you should go home. Back to Fairlane."

"But I don't want to go without you."

"Prue, I don't want to hurt you anymore, and I know that I am." One hand clasped mine and squeezed. "I see how much it hurts when I can't talk to you. I hate to do this to you, but I need to do this on my own."

"But…"

"I need to do this my way. To keep my pride." He looked up at me with his puppy dog eyes, and I knew I'd give him what he wanted, even if I didn't want to. "It might not make sense to you."

"It doesn't. I want to be here with you, to support you. I never meant to wound your pride." I teared up.

"Baby, you didn't wound my pride. I'm doing that all on my own. I hate you seeing me stuck in this bed. Once the rest of my body heals, my therapy is going to start, and I'm going to get fitted for my prosthetic. I don't know how to make you understand except to tell you that this is what I need to do. I have to do this by myself."

"I hate your pride." I pouted.

Holden smiled sadly at me, making me want to cry. "I'm not doing this to hurt you, but I know that if you stay, I'll more than likely lash out at you. I don't want you to see me like that."

"But Holden," I cried, wrapping my arms around his waist. Holden rubbed up and down my back while my tears soaked his t-shirt.

"I'm not pushing you away," he murmured.

My head shot up, and I glared at him.

"Okay, I am pushing you away, but not in the same way. I promise to talk to you. We can talk on the phone and Skype or FaceTime, whatever you want, but I don't want you here to see me struggling. When I'm done, then I'll come home."

"To Fairlane?" I asked hopefully. After him asking me to leave, I wasn't sure what he counted as home.

Cupping my cheek, his lips tipped up. "Unless you don't want me any longer."

I pushed him down and hovered over him. "You're the one who's getting rid of me. Again, I might add. How do I know that once I'm gone, you won't change your mind?"

"You'll just have to trust me." He closed his eyes as his face clouded in pain.

"If you love me, don't let me go. Hold onto me. Don't shut me out. Please, Holden," I begged.

When he opened his eyes, they were shrouded in sadness. "That's not what I'm doing, Prue. In the end,

I'm trying to save us. I need you to do this for me. Let me have my pride."

If I didn't do what he needed, I knew it would blow up in my face. Even though I didn't want to leave him, I knew I had to. Men and their pride. But what about my heart?

"Fuck you and your pride," I murmured into his chest as he held me tighter. After a long minute, he pulled me up to look at him. I wanted to cry at the resolve I saw on his fac.

"I know it won't be easy, but it's for the best." When he saw the look on my face, he amended his statement. "In the long run. I promise. We'll talk every day."

"And what, you'll just show up in Fairlane someday?"

Leaning down, Holden ran his nose along mine and kissed my forehead. "I know it's not what you want, but we'll talk so it won't be a surprise. If you want, you can come back right before I come home."

"I wish we could have one night alone at the house before I have to leave. Not stolen moments between nurses coming in and out of your room. I want to touch you."

I traced the pattern of his tattooed arm as I tried to come to terms with Holden wanting me to leave. I wasn't ready to leave and be without him, but I knew that was going to be my reality.

"Even if I could leave, it's probably not a good idea."

"Why won't you let me touch you? I don't understand. You touch me. Take care of me, and yet I can't do the same for you. I thought you wanted me." I said the last on a quiet murmur.

"Fuck, Prue," he growled. "I want you more than anything. I've fantasized about you for months. Hell, years! What I'd do to you once I got you in my arms."

I'm here now.

"Then touch me. Do what you want to me."

Tears formed in his eyes before he closed the windows to his soul, locking me out, once again. "I can't."

Before I could control myself, sobs racked my body. Holden held me to his chest as I cried for the life I could have had if Holden hadn't left after high school, and I cried for him losing his leg. I cried for him pushing me away once again.

"Prue, don't cry. I hate myself for doing this to you."

Sitting up, I sucked in a deep breath as I wiped my wet cheeks, not once looking at the man before me. Getting off the bed, I gathered my purse and slipped on my flip flops.

"Do you need anything before I go?" I asked as I dug in my purse for the keys to my rental.

"Yes, I need for you to look at me," he stated remorsefully.

I knew if I didn't, I'd hate myself for leaving in a huff, but I was beyond hurt. I didn't want him to see how badly he'd hurt me, although he knew. What were a few tear streaks when I'd been crying on him only moments before? Turning to him, I steeled myself. Who knew how long it would be before I saw him again? I needed to take in his rugged face. Memorize him.

Lifting my head, I stood strong as I looked into the eyes of the only man I'd ever loved besides my father. My breath caught in my throat at the tortured look on his face.

"Baby, come here. Please, don't leave this way," Holden said gruffly, holding his hand out for me to take.

I walked slowly over to him as if I might step in quicksand if I walked too quickly. When I finally got close enough, Holden sat forward and pulled me the rest of the way to him and up onto the bed.

"Hey, everything is going to be okay." He pulled me closer and kissed my forehead. "You're the only person I want to be with and the only person I want to spend the rest of my life with. In the long run, what's another month or two?"

"I don't want to be away from you. Is that so hard to understand?" I whimpered into his neck.

"It's not." He shook his head. "I don't want to be without you either, but I also don't want you to see me struggle for the next stage of my life."

"I understand, but I hate it," I grumbled. "I hate to complain because this isn't about me, but you want me to go back home where I'll be lonely and without you."

Nuzzling my neck, Holden sighed. "Do this for me, and we can start planning a honeymoon. How does that sound?"

"Better." I placed my hand on his chest and sat back. "Are you planning on letting me touch you?"

Holden bit down on his full bottom lip causing me to do the same. He wasn't sure, but why?

"I hope to. That's all I can give you right now." He placed his hands on top of mine. "Sometimes, I wish you'd just let me be," he laughed bitterly. "I know you only ask because you're confused, and part of that is because I don't talk about it. I'm still coming to terms with my body and what it looks like now. I don't really care about the scars that are scattered all over me, but…" Tears filled his eyes as he looked down at his legs. "This is a lot. I haven't even gotten a full look at it yet. I'm not ready for you to see me like that. Does that make sense?" His eyes came to mine.

"It does." I put my arms around him and laid my head on his shoulder, squeezing him tight. "I don't have to look at your leg to touch you, but I'll respect your wishes. I don't want to make you do anything that will make you uncomfortable. I'm sorry I didn't realize it for myself." I kissed his stubbly cheek. "Thank you for telling me, and I promise to wait as long as you need."

"Christ, I sound like a chick who isn't ready to lose her virginity," he chuckled, and a little bit of light came back into his eyes.

"All the same, I love you, Holden."

"Feel better?" he asked putting his arms around me.

"Yeah, thanks. I feel like it should be me making you feel better."

"You do. I promise. Now kiss me before you go because, even though I'm asking you to leave, I'm going to miss you like crazy."

My hands snaked around his neck as I pulled him closer, our lips meeting as if for the first time.

Desperate with longing.

I was going to miss his kisses.

My wounded Marine.

The love of my life.

28

"So, let me get this straight," Alex wrinkled her brows in confusion. "Holden asked you to leave, but he's not pushing you away?" I face planted into my couch not knowing how to explain. "Hey, sit back up, chica."

Sitting up, I stared at her through my phone screen. "He doesn't want me to see him struggle, and I get that, but it still sucks that now I'm back here in Fairlane and he's in California."

"I would have stayed if I were you," she grumbled before taking a sip from a straw sticking out of her coconut.

"I thought about it, but I think it makes him feel better knowing that I can't walk in on him at any moment. You know?" I choked up and bit my bottom lip.

"Long distance is hard when you love someone. I cried almost every single night being apart from Luke. It doesn't make you weak just because you miss him. It's normal, and it will make it all the sweeter when he's finally there."

Alex admitting she cried every night was a huge step. She hated crying in front of anyone. She didn't even talk about crying.

"Did Luke know you cried all the time?"

"Oh, hell no." She laughed, shaking her head. "Well, not until Mason told him. Luke only knew of a few times when I was at my weakest. Now, I don't let that man out of my sight, so no more crying for me," she joked.

"And where is Mr. Sandström?"

Alex sat up from her lounge chair with a smile. The next thing I knew, I had a view of the ocean with a sun-kissed Viking throwing a black-haired, equally tanned boy into the water. "He went down to play with Mason when you called. You should have come here instead of heading home. We'd be happy to have you."

"I didn't even think about it. I was on autopilot after Holden asked me to leave. I know I'm being stupid about this, but I thought once he finally let me see him, we'd be together. Does Luke have some weird male pride thing?"

Deep down, I understood Holden wanting to do everything on his own. He wanted me to see him as the strong man he was and not the one stuck in a hospital bed. It still didn't hurt any less being apart from him.

Alex tilted her head to the side as she thought about it. "Not really. He's more chivalrous. He opens doors for me, carries stuff for me, and whether he's there or not, he likes to pay for things. That's his pride. He's pretty mellow."

"Holden used to do that. I don't even know what he's like anymore in that sense. I only know the man on the other end of email and Skype."

Alex smiled assuredly. "You will, just give it time. I know you'll hate to hear it, but maybe this time apart will be good for him. He can get his head screwed on right before he comes home."

"That's what I'm afraid of."

"What?"

"That he won't come home. What if he starts thinking crazy thoughts and decides he's better off without me and disappears again?

"Oh, honey, maybe you should talk to him about your fears. I think that will alleviate a lot of your problems." How had I never realized how wise she was? If it weren't for Alex, I'd be a mess.

"Probably, but I hate to put more pressure on him

to make me feel better when it should be the other way around. I mean for Christ's sake, the man lost part of his leg, and I'm worried he's going to leave me in the dust." Embarrassed, I looked down at my hands to pick at my nail.

"Hey," she called, and when I looked back at the screen, I was met with her soft smile. "You can't help how you feel, and the only way to feel better about it is to talk to Holden. I have an idea. Why don't you talk to him about how you're feeling, and then ask if you could come visit him on your way here?"

"You don't give up." I laughed.

"Wouldn't it make you feel better to see him again?" she asked with a knowing look.

"It would," I agreed. "I'll talk to him tonight when he calls."

"And then you'll come visit?"

"You act as if you're moving there. Is there something I should know?" I asked, alarmed. As my only friend, I would be devastated if she moved away.

Alex threw her head back as she laughed. "You're bored out of your mind, and there's no reason for you not to visit. You have plenty of money now. Use it!"

"We'll see. It kind of feels wrong to be hanging out on the beach while Holden is working his ass off to learn how to walk again."

"When you put it like that, it doesn't sound so great. Seriously though, talk to him. *About everything*. You'll feel better."

"I will," I agreed and promised myself I would talk to him tonight.

"Okay, call or text me to tell me when you're coming. I'll show you around, and we'll soak up the sun for a few days."

"Hey, Prue, how's it going?" Luke asked from the sidelines.

"I'm doing okay. How about you?"

Luke's face appeared from the top of the screen as he hung over it. "I'm doing great. Hanging out with my family today while I'm off work."

Swoon.

I loved that he considered Mason and Alex his family.

"You got a good one, Alex. Enjoy him, and I'll talk to you soon."

"I know," she said with her hand to her heart. "Talk soon."

After disconnecting, and with the sun setting, Atticus and I played in the backyard. During the day, it was too hot, and I had to get his doggy energy out as best as I could with the little amount of time I had before I made a lonely dinner for one. Not long after eating dinner in front of the TV, Holden FaceTimed me.

"Hey," I answered, trying to be chipper and failing miserably.

"Hey, back. What's going on?" His mouth turned down at the corners.

"I want to talk to you."

"Great because I called to talk to you," he tried to joke.

"You look good." I smiled because he did look good. He had a little color in his cheeks after being so pale since the accident. "How are you?"

"Well, I'm a little worried after seeing your face when you answered. Cut the chitchat, Prue, and talk to me."

"Well, you're certainly bossy tonight. Fine, I talked to Alex, and she encouraged me to talk to you so you can tell me I have nothing to worry about," I chuckled miserably.

"Okay, I'll try, but I'm not going to lie to you," he answered.

"That does nothing to make me feel better, Holden." Jeez, couldn't he lie to me even just a little bit? I shook my head. I had been calling this house my home, but it felt weird to call it his home too. Maybe that was part of it. "Do you have another house?"

He blinked his wide eyes. "First, no I don't have

another house. Only the one you're living in." He sighed heavily and ran his hand through his short hair. It was getting longer, and I couldn't wait to run my fingers through it. "I can understand you being afraid I'll disappear again. I did that to you once, and all I can do is promise I'll come home to you no matter where you are. It nearly wrecked me to lose you once. I'm never going to do it again."

Tears streamed down my cheeks with abandon. "I'm sorry, Holden. I feel like a bitch…"

"You're not a bitch. I want you to tell me how you feel." His voice was a soft caress. "I knew it wouldn't be easy for you to go back home, but I didn't think you would still worry I might not come back."

I bit my lip, unsure if I should say what I said next. "If you want to talk about anything, you know I'm here. I might seem a little unstable right now, but I promise I'm not. I'm here for you in any way you need."

He looked off for a moment, but when his gaze came back, he was determined. It was a different determination than before when he'd shut down on me. This one gave me hope. "I got fully checked out today, and the doctor said I'm healing quickly. He thinks they'll measure me for a new leg next week."

"That's great news." And it was in more ways than

one. Holden had finally opened up to me and mentioned his leg. It was a step. A big one.

"He said it shouldn't take too long for me to start therapy. They have something that's like a crutch but not. I don't know, he said a lot of words I didn't understand. We'll start with that and then my new leg."

"I know you're going to kick ass. It's just like working out, so you've got this."

"But what if I don't have it?" he asked quietly, his brow furrowed.

"You will. At first, it will be tough, but I know you can push past it."

"I know you're right, but…" He looked down, unsure.

"It's going to hurt, and at first you might have to do only a few minutes at a time, but you haven't lost much muscle. You'll be up and going before you know it."

"I'm glad I've got you in my corner." He smiled sweetly at me.

"Always," I vowed. "So," I drew the word out, "when I was talking to Alex, she was trying to persuade me to visit her in Hawaii. I was thinking I might go for a few days."

"You should. I know you miss her."

"Yeah, I don't know what I would have done without her help. It will be nice when she's back."

"When's she coming back?"

"I'm not really sure. She's getting married around the middle of August, and then they'll go on their honeymoon. I think they plan to be back before Mason starts school though. Probably sometime in the beginning of September." I shrugged. I knew once she was back, she'd be busy with Mason's school and Luke.

"Go see her. You deserve some fun in the sun and to see your friend."

"I was wondering if I could come see you on my way there." I threw it out there and internally cringed at the thought he might turn me down. "It would just be for a little while. I'd have to check flights and all that. I promise not to overstay my welcome."

Holden leaned forward almost touching the screen. "Prue, you know that is not how I saw you being here."

"I know, but I just want to see you for a couple of hours. I won't camp out in the waiting room or anything."

His face softened. "Even though I didn't want you here, knowing you were close made me feel better, even if I didn't want to admit it at the time."

I knew I had a huge smile on my face, and I didn't care. It felt beyond wonderful to know that he hadn't hated me during that time.

"Book your flights and let me know when you'll be here and get a hotel for a night or two."

"Really?" I gushed.

"Fuck, Prue, you make me feel heartless." He closed his eyes with a groan. "While I didn't plan to see you until I was ready to get out of this joint, I do miss you. FaceTime isn't enough."

"I agree. I'll try to get one of the first flights out there, so I won't interrupt your therapy or anything like that. I know you don't want me there for that part, and even though it's hard, I understand." I watched as a multitude of emotions clouded his handsome face. "Can I ask you something?"

"Hit me," he shot back, leaning back in his bed with one arm behind his head. His bicep muscle bulged from the action; an ache formed between my thighs.

"Do you still have your wedding ring?" I'd been wondering if it had gotten lost or was somewhere else, but I wanted him to wear his ring.

"Yeah, I'm wearing it." He flashed me his left hand with one side of his mouth tipped up.

"You know I love you, right?" I asked, tears stinging the backs of my eyes. My insecurities about Holden not coming home to me evolved into happiness. I was ready to tackle this one last battle to be with my man.

"More than anything. I know you love me just as I love you. I couldn't have gotten through any of this without you. You know that, right?" My heartrate jumped at his sincere smile. "Now, go book your flights and let me know when I can expect you."

"Yes, sir."

I disconnected and stomped my feet in a happy dance on the floor.

I'd never been so glad to let him go. I was going to see him soon. I couldn't contain my joy as I squealed and hugged Atticus to my chest.

29

Closing my eyes, I waited for Prue to answer her phone. I wasn't sure if she'd have it on her or not, but I desperately needed to talk to her. It was my second day of therapy, and it had been brutal. My leg was rubbed raw in places from the prosthetic and throbbed from use.

I needed to see her smiling face to remind me what I was fighting for because, after the day I'd had, I was ready to stay an invalid confined to my bed. Technically, I knew I wasn't confined to my bed. I could get around with crutches and the iWalk, but I knew I wouldn't feel as if I'd succeeded until I could walk properly with my prosthetic. Even though I felt like giving up, I knew I needed to fight because I had Prue waiting for me to finally start our life, and I couldn't let her down. I'd done that enough in the past.

"Hey," she answered with a bright smile, "I didn't expect to hear from you yet."

Rubbing my hand down my face, I croaked out. "It's good to see your face."

She tilted her head for a moment and then said something to someone else before she walked for a few moments and then sat down under an umbrella. Her sweet face scrunched up in worry. "Tough day?"

"What makes you say that?"

"Uh, maybe because you've got a scowl on your face."

Fuck. I guess I hadn't been doing a good job of masking the pain.

"Maybe I just like seeing your pretty face." I tried a different tactic.

"That may be the case, Holden Montgomery, but you can't bullshit me. I've known you for too long. Spill," she demanded.

"Where are you?" I deflected, hoping it would work.

She gave me a look that said she knew what I was doing but let it slide. "I'm at the beach sitting under an umbrella. Alex was right; this place is paradise." Her smiled faded. "I wish you were here."

"Me too." I sighed as I took her in. Her cheeks were bronzed from the sun she'd already gotten. Her eyes were bright with happiness. The change was notable, and I realized she'd been alone for far too long.

"Once Mason goes to bed," she whispered and then looked over her shoulder, "and Luke comes home, I have to make myself scarce. They are all over each other," she giggled. "I didn't know what to do with myself last night. I ended up outside by the pool listening to the ocean. Isn't it weird to have a pool right next to the ocean?"

"Never really thought about it, but I guess." I laughed quietly, already feeling lighter listening to her voice and giggle.

"Well, it was actually quite peaceful. I didn't want to go down to the beach and get abducted or anything, so I got into the pool and was shocked I could hear the waves. It was nice and soothing. I think you'd like it."

"I'd like anywhere you are." I wasn't sure about getting in the ocean or pool. Maybe someday at home, but definitely not in public. I wasn't sure if I'd ever be ready for that.

Her face softened, and her smile grew as she cooed. "You can be so sweet."

"It sucks they're making you uncomfortable. Maybe you should get your own place to stay."

"The point was to be with people. What good is me

coming here if I'm holed up somewhere by myself? Their hotel didn't have any rooms available because of the movie, and I don't want to have to spend all my time going back and forth. I'll be fine. I've got my headphones, and I can go down to the pool."

"I don't want you to be uncomfortable." I could feel my brows pull tighter.

She shrugged. "It wasn't that bad, but I wanted to give them their privacy." Her eyes grew wide. "It's kind of crazy that I'm staying in a movie star's hotel suite. He seems so normal."

I couldn't help but laugh. "I'm sure he is. Just because you get a big paycheck doesn't mean you turn into someone else."

"I guess so. He's just so…never mind," her cheeks flushed pink. "Tell me about your day. Did you have therapy?"

What had she been about to say? "Do I need to be worried?" I half joked. It wasn't the first time the thought had occurred to me.

Her face turned red for the opposite reason. "Don't you start that shit with me, Holden," she growled. Jumping up she took off down the beach.

I put the hand not holding up the phone up in surrender. "I was joking. Why are you getting so defensive?"

"Maybe because I've loved you and only you forever." She stopped and glared at me. I knew her hand was on her hip even though I couldn't see it. "I just told you about how Luke and Alex can't keep their hands off each other. That was a shit thing to say."

"Prue, calm down. It's fine if you're attracted to him." And I had just said the wrong thing. Again.

"Really? Is it?" she fumed. "Are you attracted to someone else? Do I need to worry about a nurse there putting moves on my husband? Or you falling for one who'd taking care of you? Is that why you wanted me gone?" Prue had always had a jealous streak in her, and I had added fuel to the fire.

Looking down, I took a deep breath, scrubbing my hand down my face. I had gotten myself into this mess, and now it was time for me to try to dig myself out of it. "Baby, you know none of that is true. I've only ever had eyes for you. I saw what that Luke guy looked like that first day at your house, and I can't blame you if you think he's attractive. That's all. I know you'd never act on it, and neither would he. I'm sorry."

Her eyes glistened, and I knew it wasn't from the sun reflecting off the water. I was such an asshole. "Prue, I love you and only you. I'd never break our marriage vows. You know me better than that. Take a deep breath and clear your mind for a minute."

Prue could be so docile most of the time, but if she had an inkling that some woman had been interested in me in high school, she'd turned into a badass ready to kick ass and take names.

"You take a deep breath," she sassed back, but I saw the fight leave her eyes. "I don't like the fact that you can still bring out the insecure girl in me," she whispered with a frown marring her face.

"I'm sorry. It shows that you care, and I do like that." My voice softened as I tried to calm her down.

"You're sick, Holden. It should be enough that I married you and love you."

"It is," I assured her. "I didn't do it on purpose. I promise." I told her the truth and turned away so I wouldn't have to see her face. I laid it out there for her to hear. "I do worry that you'll realize I'm not enough for you and that a simple attraction to someone else could become more."

"Holden," she called my name softly, "that's never going to happen. I think if we spent more than a day here and a day there with each other, we'd feel better. *You'll* feel better once you're out of the hospital and realize that life isn't as hard as you thought it was going to be, and that I'll be there every step of the way if you let me."

She made a good point. "You're probably right about spending time together out in the real world."

"And maybe…" She hesitated, biting on her bottom lip.

"What? You can tell me."

Prue gave a little scoff. "I was going to say maybe if you'd talk to me and tell me what and how you're feeling, you'd feel better."

"It makes me feel like a pussy," I grumbled.

"You didn't used to have a problem with talking to me and expressing how you felt," she said softly, her eyes turning sad.

"I was a stupid kid back then who didn't have any problems. Now…" I choked on the word.

"Now?"

"Now, I think if I don't talk about them, they aren't true, or I can deny them a little longer." I grumbled bitterly. "I thought if I made it through my deployment, I'd come home and get the girl. And once I got you, I was going to get you pregnant and have a bunch of little Prue's running around." I shook my head at how wrong I had been. "Now…" I shrugged, uncertain if I'd ever reach my dream.

"Now, it's just going to take a little while longer. You'll get there. *We'll* get there." I could feel the conviction of her words through our connection.

"Prue," I uttered her name so seriously her head swung up, her eyes blazing, "what if you don't like who I am now?"

213

"I like everything about you, Holden. Except when you don't talk to me. As long as you let me in, we'll be fine. I meant my vows when I said them." Her eyes grew big. "I've got it! We should renew our vows. Then we'll both know it was done for the right reasons."

"I'd marry you again, or a thousand times." My lips tipped up. I'd marry her every day if she'd let me.

"Good. It's a date. I'm going to guess from all the avoidance that today didn't go well."

"You hit the nail on the head. If it weren't for you, I'd probably have given up. It was…excruciating," I closed my eyes and melted into the hard bed. "I knew it would be hard." I opened my eyes for her to see the truth. "That's why I don't want you here. For the most part, I've been pretty drugged, so I don't feel much, but today the painkillers didn't work against all the rubbing and pressure. The bad part is I know it's only going to get worse."

I watched as a tear slipped down her cheek.

"I wanted to give up until l thought about you and how you're waiting on me. Is that open enough?"

"It was perfect," she choked out. "I want you to listen to me, okay?" She waited for me to answer so I nodded. "I will wait forever for you. I'm not going anywhere. I'd be there if you let me." She gave me a mocking glare. "Knowing that, don't push yourself too hard. Take all the time you need. It's not going to happen overnight."

"I fucking love you, Prue. So damn much. You don't deserve this."

"Neither do you."

"And Holden," she brought me out of my musings, "I love you too."

30

PRUE

Late September

WATCHING OUT OVER THE YARD, MY GAZE FOLLOWED Mason as he chased Atticus, laughing each time he unsuccessfully tried to catch him.

"Are you letting him tire himself out so you can get it on with your man?" I glanced over to Alex as she sipped on her drink. Mason had been running around my backyard for at least thirty minutes.

She shrugged. "He's having fun, but I bet before we get home, he'll be asking for a puppy for his birthday. And if we waited until Mason was worn out, we'd never have sex."

Out of the corner of my eye, I saw Luke smirk before he hid it by taking a sip of his beer.

"You should get him a dog. It would help wear him out," I laughed as her cheeks reddened.

"I don't know. Would we take a dog with us when we're in LA for the summers?"

"I don't see why not, but if you ever need someone to watch your dog, I can always do it. I owe you like a gazillion favors."

Alex waved her hand at me. "Please, you don't owe me anything."

"When is your…" Luke looked to Alex for guidance, but she was too busy petting Atticus after he jumped up on her lounger. "Holden…" He raised a brow. "Isn't he supposed to be home soon?"

Tears burned the backs of my eyes, and I looked away.

"Luke," Alex scolded before putting her arm around me. "I'm sorry, Prue. He doesn't know. Obviously."

"It's okay." I tried to smile at her. "He's supposed to be coming home soon. I thought maybe by the end of next week, but…" I choked on my words.

"Fuck, Prue, I'm sorry. I didn't mean to make you cry." Luke's eyes widened with alarm.

Alex moved to sit on my lounger with me and hugged me to her. "He still hasn't called or answered any of your messages?"

"Nothing." I wiped away my tears. "Now when I

call, it goes straight to voicemail. Why won't he answer?"

"I'm sure there's a good reason. Maybe his phone broke." Alex shrugged, and I looked at her in disbelief. "Okay, it probably didn't, but it's possible. You never know."

"What if he got out and ditched me?" I cried out.

"I seriously need to meet this man." She smiled at me. "From everything you've told me, I don't think he'd do that. How did he act the last time you talked to him?"

Taking a deep breath, I laid my head on her shoulder. "He seemed fine. Upbeat because he wasn't going to be there much longer. I told him to let me know when so I could fly out there, and after we got off the phone, it's been radio silence."

"Maybe he had a setback," Alex suggested, chewing the inside of her cheek.

"Oh God, I can't imagine how he'd take it if he did have a setback. He's been doing so well, and I'm sure he's pushing himself harder than he needs to."

"Is he still going to need therapy once he's here?" Luke asked.

"I think so. He's not very open to discussing anything about his leg, but he did mention therapy here." My chest ached for Holden, for everything he'd been through and still had to endure. No one should have to go through it, but so many soldiers and veterans did.

"It can't be easy, and as a man," Luke started, and Alex giggled at his words. He shot her a stern look but smiled instantly. I wasn't sure he could be mad at her even if he tried. "We men like to take care of our women and family. He probably feels as if he's unable to do so now."

"I know, and I'm sure he's traumatized. How could he not be? He didn't talk about what he saw over there, but I could see it in his eyes, haunting him. As much as I hate to say it, it's probably good that he's been in rehab and secluded instead of having to deal with all the stresses of the real world."

"I'm so sorry, honey. I hate that he's gone through all this and you too. I know it can't be easy, but you've done an amazing job supporting him. Did you get approved for a dog yet?"

"Not yet, but I'm hoping soon. I let them know that we would like to grant a few other veterans' dogs. You'd think that would help push our application through. Since we're willing to pay outright, it should be faster, but who knows?" I shrugged. Holden had never mentioned the dog again after the one phone call that started him talking to me once he got back. I wasn't sure if he wanted one or needed one, in all honesty, because even though he had started to talk to me about some things, there was still plenty he didn't speak of.

"At least you don't have to worry about getting jobs. That should relieve some of the stress most returning veterans go through," Alex said the last quietly, her head tilted to the side. "Who the hell is that? Luke," she called quietly, her body going rigid.

Alarmed, I swung my head to where she was looking and almost passed out. Coming toward us was Holden. He looked intimidating as he limped our way. He stood tall, his muscles rippling with each shift of his body. Wearing only jeans and a t-shirt, his tattoos gleamed in the sunlight from under the white material, making him look like a bad boy biker. He was a sight for sore eyes, and it looked as if he'd bulked up since I'd last seen him; my mouth watered and my lady parts spasmed.

With his eyes trained on me, Holden continued to make his way toward me. Each stride exhibited pure determination.

I couldn't move. My brain had short circuited. He was walking.

"Prue," Alex nudged me. "Is that?"

"Holden," I breathed.

His lips tipped up as if he heard me from all the way across the yard.

My mouth cracked into a giant grin as my heart

burst with unadulterated joy. I wasn't sure if it was a dream or not, but if it was, I never wanted to wake up. Standing on shaking legs the world around me disappeared. All I could see was Holden as he *walked* toward me. I couldn't believe my eyes. I ran to him and couldn't get there fast enough. It was like in the movies when two people run toward each other and it's in slow motion. I wanted the world to move faster so I could make sure he was real.

When there was only about a foot between us, Holden stopped, and I could see him brace himself. I wanted to throw my whole body at him, but I wasn't sure if he could take the brunt of my weight or the impact. Instead, I slowed down and threw my arms around his shoulders.

The moment my arms wrapped around his warm body, I started to sob. Strong arms enveloped me and held me close as he swayed us back and forth. It was all too much. The feel of him, his heat so close to me. The way he smelled like home even after being gone for so long. I could hear his heart pound underneath my swirling head. It seemed impossible for him to be here with me in that moment.

I pulled back and placed my hands on his stubbly cheeks. "Holden, I can't believe you're here." My lower lip quivered in disbelief. "I've been trying to call you and got nothing."

His lips tipped up, face brightening in the moment. "I know. I wanted to surprise you, but I didn't count on losing my charger and my phone going dead. Getting here was a bit of an experience, but I made it. Are you surprised?" He knew I was surprised. So much so I thought it was all a dream.

"Surprised doesn't even cover it." I still had tears streaming down my cheeks as I stared up at him with a smile on my face that made my cheeks ache. "I missed you so much. Oh God, I feel like I'm going to explode, I'm so happy."

"We can't have that." He grinned full out. "Come here, I need to kiss you."

There was no way I was going to deny him. Wrapping my arms around his neck, I pulled him down for our lips to meet. I didn't expect our kiss to start off so tender. It had been too long since I'd last kissed him. His lips brushed across mine feather-light. His thumb swept over my cheek as his mouth moved ever so slowly. I'd forgotten how soft his lips were, but now that he was here, I planned to rectify that.

I gasped as his tongue slipped over my bottom lip; the ache between my legs grew. When our tongues finally touched, I let out a moan. A thrum of desire shot straight through my body. His long fingers wrapped around the strands of my hair, pulling me the way he wanted me. Giving him better access. I slipped one hand down to press against his rock-hard chest as the other scraped along his scalp.

"Maybe we should leave them alone," I heard in the faint distance.

"That's hot," Alex murmured.

"I'll show you hot," Luke growled.

Holden pulled away, amusement written all over his face. His voice was full of gravel when he spoke. "I need to be alone with you."

Face planting into his chest, I softly said, "I couldn't agree more." Pulling back, I reached up on tippy-toes and placed a chaste kiss on the lips I'd been dreaming about for the past few months.

Before I got lost in Holden again, I turned around to our guests with a bright smile on my face. "In case you haven't guessed, Alex and Luke, this is Holden."

"It's really nice to meet the man who's put that smile on her face," Alex greeted.

Holden ducked his head. "Thank you, both of you, for everything you've done to help Prue. It means a lot to me to know she's had good people backing her up."

Luke stepped forward and they did a weird man hug thing. I think Holden was a little taken aback by the gesture. "Thank you for your service. It's great to see you under better circumstances."

"Yeah, I guess I didn't make the best first impression, did I?" Holden wrapped his arm around my waist.

I wanted to swoon. Everything seemed so normal and yet so surreal. It was nothing like the last time I'd seen Holden.

"That's okay. We all go a little crazy sometimes for the women we love." Luke smiled. Apparently, their meeting that morning on my front porch forgiven.

"Thanks, man." A chuckle escaped. "I was a little crazy. I hate to be rude, but it's been too long since I last saw my wife."

My heart rate picked up at the word wife and my stomach fluttered. My love for him was endless and I couldn't wait to be alone with him. I was too overwhelmed to hear what else was said. I stood dreamy-eyed as they spoke until Alex gave me a big hug, her smile wide. "I'll talk to you soon. No rush, you've got some making up to do," she whispered in my ear.

"Thank you. I can't believe he's here." I squeezed her harder.

"It was a great surprise. I'm glad he's finally home. Go be with your man and get him settled in."

Holden and I stood side-by-side while we watched Luke, Alex, and Mason leave with Atticus trying to follow. Once they were out of sight, I laced my fingers with Holden's and led him up to the house. I stood at the back door and turned to Holden, and the moment I faced him, his lips crashed into mine. We were all tongues and teeth as we devoured each other. Gone was the tenderness from earlier. We were desperate for each other.

"Welcome home, Mr. Montgomery," I breathed against his lips.

"It's good to be home, Mrs. Montgomery."

31

PRUE

Smiling wide, I slowly dragged Holden inside the house. I still couldn't believe he was finally here, and that he had surprised me in the best possible way. I couldn't help but continue to glance back at him every few seconds to make sure he was real and admire how handsome he was. When we were in high school, I'd thought no one could be as good looking as he was, but damn he was fine now. Manhood suited him. Holden took everything in as he let me lead him through the house and into the bedroom.

"Prue." My core clenched from that one husky word alone.

Stopping in front of the bed, I placed my hands on his rock-hard chest. My fingers trailed down to the hem of his shirt and slowly started to lift it over his head but stopped dead in their tracks at the tattoo on Holden's chest. My eyes flicked up to his and then back down.

"Holden," I gasped, my hand going over mouth, "when did you get this?"

"The day I enlisted in the Marines." He swallowed roughly, his eyes boring into mine.

"Why didn't you say anything?" My fingertip traced over the letters of my name that graced his left pectoral muscle.

"What did you want me to say? That I've loved you all these years, and to prove it, my first tattoo was of your name. I wanted it to be a surprise. Now, can we get this shirt off me? I'd like to touch you," he said impatiently as he peeked over his shirt, arms still in the air.

"Yes, of course, I was taken aback by my name on your body. I can't believe you did that." I tore his shirt off the rest of the way and went back to staring at his chest. I kind of wanted to get his name inked on my skin like it was stamped on my heart.

His hands came to my waist, pulling me closer until our bodies were flush. Mine melted against his as my arms circled around his neck.

"I need you naked," he growled. His head dipped, and his lips skated down the column of my neck. Pulling my shirt off, his heated gazed intensified as he took in my lace covered breasts. His hands skimmed down my torso. The feel of his touch on me made my core throb with need. Pulling down my shorts, I stood before him in only my bra and panties. Thank God I'd worn a sexy pair today, and I knew Holden approved by the desire in his eyes and the hardness pressed into my stomach. All I could think about was how much I wanted to feel it in my hands and wrap my lips around his length, tasting his salty goodness.

"Fuck, Prue, when you look at me like that, I want to devour you," he moaned from deep in his throat. "It's been too long."

With shaky fingers, I popped the button on his jeans and slowly undid the zipper. "Let me take care of you."

"Please," his head fell forward, chin to his chest, as he watched my every move.

My hand slipped inside and met velvety steel. Pulling his thick length out, my mouth watered at the sight before me. Slipping my hands around to his ass, I pulled his jeans and boxer briefs down his legs until I got to just above his knees. Looking up, I waited for some clue as to what he wanted me to do, but his eyes were clenched tight.

"Sit on the bed," I murmured, placing a kiss on the tattoo that covered his heart.

Doing what I asked, Holden slowly sat down and then looked up at me with uneasy eyes.

Slowly I bent, taking off his shoes and getting my

first look at the metal that now replaced part of his left leg. It wasn't anything I hadn't seen before, and I knew what to expect. I'd done a lot of research these past months. The only surprise was how easily Holden bared himself to me. I paid no mind to the prosthetic as I pulled his jeans and boxers the rest of the way off.

My hands smoothed their way up his muscular thighs, feeling the course hair until they met the juncture of his pelvis. One hand went to his waiting cock and the other gripped his hip. His dick twitched at my touch, and I couldn't wait to give him more. His hips jerked up as I licked across his slit and swirled my tongue around his tip. Sucking him into my mouth, I bobbed up and down as far as I could go, letting my hand take over the rest.

One of his hands fisted in my hair, the other going to the comforter and gripping it tightly. "Fuck, Prue, I've missed your hot mouth. Take me all the way down your throat. Open for me, baby."

Out of practice, I did the best I could. I took him in until he hit the back of my throat and then swallowed him down until my lips met the base of his cock. "That's it," he called, using one hand to set the pace as he fucked my mouth. He moaned as my hand reached around and cupped his balls; he swelled in my mouth.

"Oh God, Prue, I'm going to come." He stilled my head, pushing his hips up and spilled down my throat.

Pulse after pulse of his essence shot out before his body went lax. "Come here," he called, pulling me up and onto his lap. With his eyes closed, Holden rested his forehead against mine. "I needed that. I was too wound up to properly take care of you."

"Mmm," I hummed, intoxicated by being in his arms. Kissing his chin, I grinned. "We do need to consummate this marriage."

"Oh, we will my sweet wife, but first I need to taste you. Crawl up there and let me have my way with you." His eyes flashed fire, and my core pulsed.

As I crawled up the bed, I panted in anticipation of Holden touching me after being apart for so long. Every night in my dreams, he touched me, but it wasn't as good as the real thing. Nothing was as good as Holden's mouth and hands on me.

"Right there," he growled out and bit my ass cheek; I squealed. "Stay like that. I want to eat you just like that with your beautiful ass on full display." His nose dragged down from the middle of my back, every once in a while stopping to place a tender kiss. When he hit my crack and trailed down, I shivered in delight. Pushing aside my panties, one finger slipped through my folds. His long digit dipped inside, and instantly I needed more. I reared back but he stopped me with another bite to my other cheek.

"Be patient. We've got all night. Let me show you how much I've missed you all these years."

His hot tongue swept up and down my slit. Pushing inside only to lick up to my bundle of nerves and swirl his tongue around. He continued to repeat this pattern until I couldn't take it anymore.

"Holden, please, fuck me," I moaned out in frustration. My hands clung to the comforter beneath me.

Two fingers filled me, pumping, building me back up before retreating. I wanted to cry until those very same fingers moved to my clit. Using my juices, Holden rubbed small circles on my nub as his hot tongue fucked my core. Higher and higher, I built. Pushing back against his face for more, I fell over the edge. My world shattered around me as I fell face first into the bed, panting. My ass still in the air, Holden held me there, licking up every drop of my orgasm. I writhed against his face as I slowly came down.

When my breathing finally calmed, Holden snuggled up beside me. His arm wrapped around my waist as he placed kisses on every inch of skin he could reach.

"That was amazing," I finally said, lacing my fingers with his.

"You're fucking beautiful when you come."

"You couldn't even see my face," I laughed.

"Your pussy is beautiful when you come. It's missed me." He lightly bit down on my shoulder.

I squirmed, pressing my ass against his hard cock; Holden moaned and pulled me tighter against him. "I've missed you. Not just these past few months, but for years, I've longed for you to be right where you are now."

"I promise to make up for all the years I was gone. Starting now," he growled, rolling me over and pinning me under him.

My hands moved to his sides and ran up the taut ridges of his stomach and the few spots of puckered skin—scars from where shrapnel from the IED had hit him—only stopping once my hand was over what I now dubbed 'my tattoo.'

"You really like it don't you?"

"Yes." I scratched my nails down his torso until I came into contact with his hot length. Wrapping my hand around his cock, I pulled him closer until his lips were only a breath away.

"Good, it was a way for me to keep a little piece of you with me always."

My heart melted, and I forgave him for leaving me all those years ago. I knew deep down he thought he was doing what was best for the both of us. He was so young. Did I like what he'd done? No, but we were together now, and I knew nothing was going to tear us apart again.

I leaned up, capturing his lips in a searing kiss.

Tasting my juices still covering his full, kissable lips, I wanted him again. Pulling back, Holden skated his hand between my breasts until he reached my core. His thumb rubbed rough circles as my hips bucked up against him. "I need to be inside of you. Are you ready for me?" He dipped two fingers inside and pumped once before removing them.

Rubbing up and down my slick core, Holden coated his dick until it glistened with my arousal. His cock was beautiful and even more so when it was coated with me. Once he was satisfied, he slowly pushed his way in.

I couldn't help but close my eyes as he filled and stretched me. It felt so good. Like finally feeling whole after years of missing a part of me. I was so full, and when I thought I couldn't take anymore, he pulled almost all the way out, stilling. Wrapping my legs around his lean hips, I licked up his neck as I pulled him back in with my legs. When I bit down on his earlobe, Holden groaned loudly, picking up his pace. His hips pounded into mine as his thumb continued to rub delicious circles around my clit. His pace was dizzying, or maybe it was the feel of him finally being inside of me after all this time. I wasn't sure which, and I didn't care. My only thought was that I never wanted it to end.

"Fuck, Prue, I need you to come. I don't think I can

hold on much longer. You're so fucking tight," he gritted out. Leaning down, he plunged his tongue into my waiting mouth. His tongue mimicked what his hips were doing, and with one pinch to my clit, I flew over the edge, pulling him right along with me. I felt his dick pulse each time I clenched him, milking him of his hot semen.

Holden collapsed on top of me, panting into my neck. My arms wrapped around him, caressing the expanse of his broad back. As his breath slowly calmed, and he rolled to his side and wrapped me in his arms. "I missed you so fucking much."

"I missed you too. I thought I knew how much until I saw you walking toward me."

Our hands wandered and caressed as we laid there enjoying being in each other's arms, talking about little things. There had been very little privacy back when we'd been in high school, and we'd never gotten a chance to really enjoy each other like this before. I treasured being able to stay in his arms for hours if I wanted to. Being able to show him how much I loved him with my body and touch alone. When I heard his stomach growl, I couldn't help but laugh as mine echoed it.

"You're hungry. I can make us something to eat."

"I could eat. What do we have?"

"Nothing exciting. If I'd known you were coming home, I would have gone to the store. I can make you a sandwich, or I have some left-over lasagna in the fridge I can heat up."

Holden's eyes lit up at the word home, and I loved it. He'd lived too long without one, and I was determined to make him feel like this was his home too.

He groaned and dipped to kiss me on the nose. "Lasagna sounds wonderful. Did you make it?" he asked excitedly.

"I did." I smiled, remembering how much he used to love eating my lasagna. "I'll go heat some up and meet you back in here. I'm not sure if I'm done with you."

His brown eyes turned into dark with lust. "You better go before I spend another two hours having my wicked way with you."

I scurried off the bed, throwing on the shirt Holden had worn earlier, and made my way to the kitchen. Cutting a large piece for him and a much smaller piece for myself, I placed them in the toaster oven while I got him a glass of milk and me a sweet tea.

When I got back to the bedroom, Holden was sitting up against the headboard with his eyes closed and a serene look on his handsome face. He looked at peace. I couldn't help but stand there taking him in. He wasn't my cute boyfriend from high school anymore.

No, now Holden was rugged and handsome. He was all man with his lean face and carved-out-of-stone jaw. His chest was still slightly tanned with bulging muscles that I had enjoyed watching ripple as he fucked me. Then there were the tattoos. Tribal tattoos covered his arms, chest, and back. The only one out of place was my name. I wanted to trace each and every inch of his ink with my tongue.

"Are you going to stand there all night or are you going to feed me?" he asked with his eyes still closed.

"How?"

"My stomach started growling non-stop the second I smelled your lasagna. Stop denying me woman and feed me," he growled playfully.

Walking to the bed, I laughed. "They always say the way to a man's heart is through his stomach. I think you fell in love with me because of my lasagna."

"There are a lot of things that made me fall in love with you, but right now your lasagna will reaffirm my love."

"Maybe I should feed you too?" I questioned with a raised brow.

"Now, no need for all that. Maybe you can just blow on it for me."

Laughing, I sat our plates down and kissed him on the cheek. "I missed your sense of humor."

"I'll be here all…forever. Shit," he laughed, taking

a sip of his milk, "that didn't sound good, but neither does all week. You know what I mean."

"Don't worry about it. Just eat so I can have my way with you again."

"Yes, ma'am." He saluted me.

"Holden?" I said his name quietly, unsure if he was asleep yet or not.

"Mmm…" He pulled me closer to his chest and nuzzled me.

"Can I ask you something?"

"Of course, anything." He kissed the top of my head.

"You were or are surprisingly okay with me seeing your body and your leg."

"That's not a question." His voice was monotone. I wasn't sure if I should continue or not, but I knew if I held back everything I wanted to say to him, I'd start to resent him and myself. I wanted us to be able to communicate.

"No, I guess it's not, but I don't know, I thought it would be tougher to get you into bed with me. You would barely let me touch you when I saw you before. What happened?" I thought he'd be more uncomfortable and would want the lights out. That he'd hide from me.

"Well," he drew out the word, "I've had plenty of time to think these past few months, and I realized I'd be the dumbest man on the planet if, after finally winning you back, I lost you because I was ashamed of my body. My leg isn't ever going to grow back, and while it was hard, I knew I had to come to terms with the way my life is now." He squeezed me tighter. "I have so much to be thankful for. I shouldn't have to get any more surgeries, and I'm lucky I lost my leg where I did. I realized it's not the end of the world. This is who I am now."

I leaned up on my elbows to look down at him. "I was afraid of how you saw yourself in the hospital. I know it was hard when you couldn't get out of bed because your body needed to heal. You really are lucky."

"Not once when you were visiting did you look at me differently."

"Of course not, Holden. I love you, and I'm grateful you're here with me. You're still you. Hell, you're better than you were in high school. You're the new and improved Holden Montgomery. Only now you're a little bionic."

Holden threw his head back and laughed. "I'm not

bionic yet but maybe one day." His face turned serious, his eyes searching mine. "It really doesn't bother you?"

"Not one bit."

"You haven't seen it without the sock on it. You might change your mind," he mumbled, not looking my way.

Sitting up I looked him in the eyes. "Do you think I'll see it and all of a sudden ask for a divorce? When you're ready for me to look, then I'll look, but it's not going to change the way I feel about you. I can promise you that."

"It happens," he replied, looking up at the ceiling.

Taking a breath, I nodded because it did happen. "I'm sure it does. Not everyone is as lucky as you. So many more are hurt so badly, but I truly believe this will barely change your life.

"I'm so lucky to have you by my side. If you weren't so understanding, I wouldn't be where I am today. More than likely, I would have gone into a deep depression, so thank you for sticking with me even when I was an asshole and pushed you away."

"You're welcome." I kissed my name on his chest.

"I'm not going to lie. Not all days are good days, but I know I can do this. I have a therapist to see in Riverside to help me deal with everything. I only ask for you to be patient with me."

"I promise." He had no idea what I'd go through to

be with him. There was no way I'd ever let him leave me again.

"With you, the most beautiful woman in the world, by my side, I can get through anything."

"And I promise I'll never leave your side. Not until the end of my days."

32

PRUE

Two Years Later

"HOLDEN, YOU'VE GOT TO LET ME UP. THE GIRLS ARE waiting for me." I writhed underneath him. His hot mouth trailed kisses down my stomach.

Looking up at me through his lashes, he smiled. "I want you to come for me one more time. Then you can go."

"I'm already late. Do you want to get married today or not?"

His brows pulled together. "It's a vow renewal, and we're already on our honeymoon. I don't see what the big deal is. One more orgasm. You know you want it. Later, you'll be dying for my mouth on your hot body."

"Maybe the fact that we asked our friends to come with us to celebrate, and they're waiting," I moaned as he slipped a long digit into my core and curled it, hitting me in that special spot that drove me wild. Holden had woken me up bright and early, nestled between my legs, and so far, hadn't come up for air. Not that I was complaining. Well, I was, but not for that reason.

"I can paint your nails for you later if you want. Right now, I want to devour your pussy." He smirked up at me.

"For the love of all that's holy, you are not painting my nails. Don't you want to hang out with the guys?" I moaned when his mouth moved to my clit and sucked.

Holden's head popped up. "Are you really asking me that?" He plunged his fingers deep inside and massaged in just the right place. "I'd much rather be here with you, but I promise to let you go after you come once more."

"Then I want you to fuck me. I need to feel you inside of me. Please, Holden, don't deny me." My hips ground against his hand, moving with the tempo of his fingers. I was getting close, and I wanted to be full of him.

Kissing up my body, Holden nipped my bottom lip. "When have I ever denied you?"

"Never," I answered breathily.

"That's right, baby, now since you're trying to hurry me along, I want you to ride me. Do you think you can do that?" He licked along my bottom lip only to fuck my mouth with his tongue. He plunged deep and swirled his tongue with mine, not stopping until we were both out of breath and gasping for air.

His hot length rested high on my thigh, but not where I needed it most. With my hands to his chest, I pushed him to the side and took advantage, straddling him. I rubbed my core up and down his long cock, but I needed more. So much more. Wrapping my hand around his thick shaft, I slowly lowered myself onto him. Inch by glorious inch, he was right where I needed him to be.

"That's right, baby, just like that. Take me all the way in. Fuck, Prue, how are you always so tight and ready for me?" he groaned out, biting his bottom lip and driving me wild.

Leaning down, I bit his bottom lip, pulling it from between his teeth, and then sucked on it. Hard. My hips started to rock and, on the way down, I rubbed my clit into his pelvis. My already sensitive nub had me halfway there as I rode him with abandon. Leaning back, I placed my hands on his thighs as I opened myself up for him, feeling every inch as I took him in. One hand massaged and pinched my breast, as Holden's thumb rubbed me in slow circles.

"Oh God, I'm so close," I moaned, riding him faster.

"Let yourself go. Milk my cock, baby. I want to feel you squeeze every last drop out of me."

And I did just that. I let loose and flew. Pleasure and fireworks erupted until I couldn't move any longer. I collapsed on his chest, placing a kiss on my tattoo. Holden took over, hands on my hips as he moved me up and down drawing out his own orgasm. He moaned into my neck, his fingertips digging deep into my ass. Biting down on my neck, he released. Thrusting one last time deep inside of me.

I wrapped my arms and legs around my husband. We had come a long way since he'd showed up at my father's funeral. Some days, I still wasn't sure how he convinced me to marry him. I must have been in shock, but not once had I ever regretted it. I had tried to push him away, to stay mad at him after he'd left again, but each email he'd sent me was a jolt to my heart that slowly started to warm it up after years of being shut down. Each and every day, Holden let me know how much he loved me and how grateful he was that I hadn't let him push me away after his accident. There were more than a few bad days over the past couple of years, but we had worked through them. Holden talked to me and his therapist along with his new friends, Luke, Jax, and Jack. I was proud of him and how much he'd overcome. Now, unless you knew him, you'd never know he wore a prosthetic.

Holden was simply the best thing that had ever happened to me.

"With your hormones lately, I thought you'd want to stay in bed all day," Holden rasped into my ear, bringing me to the here and now.

"I didn't say I didn't want to. Only that I couldn't. I can't leave the girls waiting for me all day."

"Well," he chuckled, "they should have waited until you called. It *is* our honeymoon."

"True, but every day is our honeymoon. Anyway, I wasn't thinking when we made the plans. After this, it's just you and me, and I can promise you I won't let you out of bed for the next," I swayed my head from side to side, "three months or so."

"I'd better take my vitamins then." He laughed, smoothing his hand down my back.

"Probably wise, Mr. Montgomery. Now, I really should go. They're going to think you fucked me unconscious and will come storming through our door any minute now."

The girls—Alex, Gabi, and Taylor—had barely seen me since we had all landed in Bora Bora for our Christmas vacation/honeymoon. I was sure they'd been busy with their own husbands, but I couldn't get enough of mine. Who knew getting pregnant increased your libido so much? I certainly didn't, but Holden was gladly reaping the benefits. In fact, he liked it so much that I was pretty sure he was going to try to have me pregnant as much as possible.

"They know I'd let you up for air and to eat. I can't let you wither away on me. Let me say goodbye to peanut first, and then you can go." He nuzzled my neck. Sliding down my body, Holden kissed my little bump. "Daddy loves you, peanut. We'll talk more later." With one last kiss, he sat up in all his naked glory.

Even with the four orgasms of the morning, I was ready for more. Holden worked out religiously. So much so, instead of going to the gym, we now had one at our house. He kept his body strong. He always had, but now it was more important since it made his life so much easier. His body was insane. All I had to do was look at him, and I wanted to jump him and ride him until next week. He was a natural aphrodisiac.

"Don't look at me like you want to devour me," he said shaking his head with a chuckle. "You have to go."

"I know." I pouted. "What are you going to do while I'm gone?"

He sat on the edge of the bed, slipping on his leg. "Luke's having us all over to his bungalow to watch a soccer game. I'm sure there will be plenty of beer and yelling."

"Sounds like fun." It didn't, and Holden knew it. I pretty much disliked watching any sport but football. It must have been from watching him play so much in high school. Most of the time, when the guys got together to watch sports, the girls and I drank and talked. It was a win-win for everyone.

I slipped on a light-yellow sheath dress along with a pair of flip-flops and pulled my hair up into a ponytail. I didn't need to do much since I was meeting the girls for a spa day for mani-pedis, massages, and facials. All to get ready for our sunset vow renewal.

Grabbing my phone and keycard, I made my way to Holden, stepping between his spread legs. His hands ran up the back of my thighs, squeezing my ass along the way before he wrapped his arms around me and hugged me to him.

"Have fun with the girls. I'll see you later. I'll be the guy under the arch thing," he murmured against me.

I couldn't help but laugh. I didn't know what it was called either, but it was pretty and romantic, and I wanted it. "And I'll be the girl in the white dress, holding the flowers."

"The prettiest girl on the beach."

Kissing the top of his head, I pulled back. "I'll see you later. I love you."

"Later. I love you too."

Before he could say or do something to make me

stay another second, I hightailed it to the door and slipped outside. When I got to the end of the wooden walkway that led to the beach, I found Alex, Gabi, and Taylor all sitting on a golf cart with drinks in their hands.

Gabi looked down at her phone and shook her head. "Only forty minutes late. Not bad," she cackled.

"Don't listen to her. We were all late and Gabi was the last to arrive." Alex raised an eyebrow at Gabi.

"Don't worry. We all know how it is," Taylor said smiling up at me. "But I guess you're already married so you should be out of the honeymoon stage."

Gabi and Alex looked at each other and started laughing. Taylor complained a lot that she wasn't getting it on the regular because her toddler still didn't want to sleep through the night. I knew both Gabi and Alex were in the same boat as me, minus the hormones, and had sex with their men as much as possible. One look at their man, and they were all over him. We couldn't help it that we were all married to extremely hot guys with bodies to rival any male model.

"I personally hope we never leave the honeymoon stage," Alex quipped, a large smile on her face letting us know she was thinking about getting down with her husband later.

"You're lucky he let me go at all. Holden even said he'd paint my nails so I didn't have to leave."

They all oohed and aahed at the sweetness as I jumped into the golf cart beside Gabi. Alex was at the wheel and only ran us off the trail once from laughing as she drove us up to the main part of the resort.

We were all lined up getting our nails done after our facials and massages. It had been a relaxing afternoon of being pampered along with a seafood lunch brought into a private lounge.

"I can't believe we have to leave tomorrow. I have to say this has been the best vacation I've ever been on," Taylor said from beside me.

"I have to agree," Gabi watched as her toenails were painted a vibrant shade of pink.

"Me too." Alex's eyes grew wide. "I have an idea. Why don't we make this a tradition? Every year for Christmas, we can either come here or go somewhere else, but we go somewhere tropical to get away from Missouri's freezing temperatures."

"Oh, I'm in." Gabi smiled wide, her eyes filled with excitement. "I'm still not used to the cold. Luckily, I have Jax to keep me warm. He's lucky I love him so much…"

"Like you'd leave Fairlane," Alex laughed at her.

Gabi shook her head in annoyance, but she had a smile on her face. We all knew she would never leave.

WALKING DOWN THE AISLE OF SCATTERED PINK ROSE petals on the beach, I caught sight of Holden. He was standing underneath the arch thing that was more a square, but no one cared. The legs and top were covered in ivy and white roses, calla lilies, and sweet peas. It was beautiful with the ocean as the backdrop. The flowers were no match for Holden who was tanned to golden perfection, wearing a linen shirt and pants. His hair was slicked back, keeping it out of his eyes. He'd let it grow out now that he could, and I loved running my fingers through it. His eyes were on me, never wavering as I walked toward the love of my life.

By the time I reached him, tears stung my eyes, but I held them back. I didn't want to miss a second of our day. When we'd gotten married by the judge, I'd been on autopilot and didn't remember a bit of it. So, this time I was committing everything to memory. The contrast to then and now was like day and night.

Taking my hand in his, Holden pulled me flush against him. His lips found mine in a searing kiss. The officiant cleared his throat as our friends laughed. "Although you're already married, you're supposed to wait until the end of the ceremony to kiss your bride."

Holden turned to the officiant with a devilish grin on his face. "I couldn't help it. She's absolutely beautiful. Don't you agree?"

"Yes, very lovely." He gave us a small smile as he shifted in place.

"Good," Holden nodded. "If you could speed up the ceremony, I'd be most grateful."

"Holden," I whispered. "It's already short. Let the man do his job. After this…"

He cut me off. "After this, I'm taking you back to our bungalow. Does anyone have any objections to that?"

"Only if you let us see her before we leave tomorrow," Alex shouted from her seat.

"Deal," he turned back to the minister. "Now, let's get this show on the road. Wait." He held his hand up. Pulling me close, Holden brought his mouth to the shell of my ear. His hot breath raked over me, sending shivers down my spine. "I just want you to know, you look so beautiful; you're glowing. Thank you for marrying me. Again."

"Holden," my voice cracked, "you're going to make me cry." I hugged him, my head tilted up so only he could hear me. "Not a day has gone by when I regretted marrying you."

"Now you're going to make me cry." He laughed, wiping at his eyes. "Okay, now you can continue. I promise we won't interrupt you again."

"Please join hands."

Holden's hands engulfed my own, and he rubbed

his thumbs over the tops in a soothing motion. I wasn't sure who he was trying to soothe, though, him or me?

"Holden, will you continue to have Prue as your wife and continue to live in this marriage?"

"I do," he vowed. And he had. From the moment, Holden had come back to Fairlane, he had been the best husband and lived in the now with me and Atticus. For all the worrying I'd done, it had been for nothing.

"Do you reaffirm your love for her, and will you love, honor, and cherish her in sickness and in health, for richer or poorer, for better or worse, forsaking all others, and be faithful to her as long as you both shall live?"

"I do."

I repeated after the officiant as I gazed into Holden's eyes. They were filled with so much happiness and love, and I knew mine mirrored his. He had been my forever since I was fifteen-years-old and always would be. We'd already been through richer and poorer, better and worse, and sickness and health. I knew there would be more tough times ahead of us, but we'd already beaten the odds and would do it again and again.

"You may now kiss your wife," the officiant announced.

Holden's face morphed into pure happiness. Pulling me by the hands, I crashed against his muscular chest, looking up at him with my own beaming smile. Our lips pressed together in a kiss I felt down to my toes as they curled into the warm sand. Holden dipped me, deepening the kiss. Our friends cheered and clapped bringing us out of our passion.

Then I felt something I'd never felt before. One of the best feelings in the entire world.

Eyes wide, I smiled as I felt the baby kick for the first time.

"Do you have any idea how beautiful you are when you smile?"

My smile grew larger. I couldn't wait for him to feel our baby.

Cupping my face in his hands, Holden placed kisses all over my face while I laughed. Turning he looked out at our friends. "We'll see you all later. I've got to go ravish my wife, and I suggest you all do the same to your wives."

All the guys hooted and hollered as they swung their wives over their shoulders and headed to their bungalows. It didn't take long for us to follow.

33

Three Years Later

"DADDY," MY DAUGHTER GIGGLED FROM BESIDE ME, looking around the kitchen. Her sweet face was covered in flour, and her hair was sticking up every which way. "We made a mess."

Cooking with Violet was always an experience, but we really had outdone ourselves in trying to make Prue a Mother's Day breakfast to beat all breakfasts. We tried, and may have failed, in making all her favorite breakfast foods. There were pancakes, scrambled eggs, French toast, hash browns, and ham. Most were either burned or undercooked, but it was made from love so hopefully, she'd forgive our lack of cooking skills.

"We'll clean it up before she sees. I promise she won't know how disastrous the kitchen is." I kissed Violet on the top of her strawberry scented head. At least I hoped Prue never knew. There was flour, oil, and eggs pretty much everywhere the eye could see. I wouldn't be surprised if we found some on the ceiling. Luckily, Atticus had helped keep the floor relatively clean. He was better than any broom or mop.

"Deal." She scrunched her brows in all seriousness.

"Holden," Prue screamed from the bedroom. It wasn't the scream of finding a huge mess in the kitchen or somewhere else in the house. She was in pain. She had sounded the exact same way when she'd gone into labor with Violet.

I was instantly on alert. "Holy sh…shabooby," I corrected myself for Violet's delicate ears. Gripping Violet by the shoulders, I sat her out of the way and darted around the island.

I ran as fast as I could to my wife to find her kneeling on the floor by our bed in a puddle of what had to have been amniotic fluid.

"Shit, Prue, are you okay?" My hand trailed up and down her back.

She looked up at me with fierce determination in her eyes, her teeth gritted together. "Get me to the fucking hospital now. I want drugs," she seethed. Even the devil himself would have been afraid of the fire in her eyes.

Prue had not received any drugs while in labor with Violet and had sworn she would never have another baby again. Obviously, she had changed her mind, but she was determined not to feel an ounce of pain this time around. It looked as if that ship had sailed, but I would try to remedy that as soon as possible.

"Call Alex now and ask her to come get Vi and help me get off the damn ground."

I had a feeling baby number two was going to be our last. Prue didn't forget a thing. She might forgive but certainly didn't forget, and the prospect of having our own basketball team wasn't looking good at the moment.

"Now, Holden," she growled out, her eyes slits as she peered up at me.

Wrapping my arm around her waist, I hoisted her up and helped her lean against the bed as I snatched up my phone and punched in Luke's number. It rang four times before he answered, sounding exhausted. "Hey man, I…"

"I need Alex to come over to the house and watch Vi. She can take her back to your house. Whatever she wants, but I need her here now. Prue's in labor."

"Holy shit!" Luke laughed, sounding more awake. "You've got to be kidding me. I'm at the hospital now with Alex. She's in labor. It happened around two this morning."

"Who am I going to call? Prue said Alex."

"Holden get off the phone and grab my bag. Do I smell something burning?" she screeched almost blowing my eardrums.

Shaking my head, I grabbed the bag she'd packed. "No, baby. Vi and I were making you breakfast for Mother's Day. Now that I think about it, I might have left the stove on. I'll be right back."

"Relax, dude, and call Gabi. She loves Violet and would be happy to watch her. Then get your ass to the hospital before Prue rips off your balls." Little did Luke know his own balls could very well be in danger. Women turned into different creatures when they were in labor, but I'd let him find that out for himself.

Heading back to the kitchen, I found Violet sitting on a stool eating a pancake and giving one to Atticus. He was her best friend. He always sat underneath her while she ate knowing he'd get a smorgasbord of food each and every day. He really was better than a broom or mop.

But I couldn't believe I'd left Violet in the room with the stove on. I scooped her into my arms, turned off the stove, and carried her back to the bedroom where Prue was waiting.

"Mommy," Violet cried out in happiness when she

spotted her mom and reached her arms out for Prue to take her. "Happy Mother's Day."

"Baby, I don't know if Mommy can…"

"Let me sit down," Prue interrupted as she hoisted herself onto the bed and held her own arms out. "Come here, sweet girl."

Once Vi was sitting on her mom's lap, Prue hugged her, nuzzling the top of her head.

"I've got to call Gabi. You'll never believe it, but Alex went into labor earlier," I said already punching in Jax's number.

With wide eyes, Prue's hand went to her stomach. "You need to tell her to hurry because this baby is coming fast," she grunted. "I can't believe Alex and I are going to have babies on the same day."

"Is my brother coming?" Vi clapped excitedly.

"Yeah, baby, he's coming." Prue tried to smile through a contraction.

"Hello," Jax answered in his usual gruff voice.

"Jax," I let out a sigh, "I need you and Gabi to come over and watch Violet for us. Prue's in labor."

"No shit," he said calmly then yelled, "Hey, baby, Prue's in labor; we've got to get over there." I heard Gabi yell, and then Jax laughed. "We'll be there as fast as we can."

"Are they coming?" Prue asked desperately. I knew she was trying to hide how much pain she was in from

Violet, but there was no hiding the tight set of her jaw.

"Yeah, just breathe, baby. They should be here in less than ten minutes."

"Easy for you to say," she snapped and instantly her face turned soft. "I'm sorry, Holden. It hurts like a son of a…you know. It's going so much quicker than with Violet. Do you think the baby's okay?"

"I'm sure he's fine. It's supposed to go quicker with your second, and now that your water broke…"

"Don't remind me. What if I don't get any drugs?" she asked with her lower lip trembling.

I didn't know what to say to appease her, so I said nothing. Instead, I sat down on the bed next to her and hugged my two girls.

Prue gripped my hand as another contraction hit and the doorbell rang.

"Violet, baby, can you go let Uncle Jax and Aunt Gabi in? They're going to stay here with you while I take your mom to the hospital so your brother can be born."

"But I want to go with you," she pouted and slumped to the floor.

"I know you do, but the hospital is not a fun place. You'll have fun with your aunt and uncle, and then after your brother is born, they'll bring you up, so you won't miss any of the fun."

"Really?" She jumped up and ran out to answer the door.

"You shouldn't have done that," Prue breathed, still clutching my hand.

"I know, but I didn't want them waiting, and I couldn't leave you in the middle of a contraction. I'll have a talk with her later about not opening the door. I promise."

Her green eyes, sparkling with tears, looked up at me. "Holden, I'm scared. This is all happening too quickly. Are you ready for this?"

"As ready as I'll ever be, but I know we've got this. Look at how well we've done with Vi. She's such a good kid."

"That means this baby will probably be the opposite," she grumbled, resting her head on my shoulder.

"Possibly, but I doubt it. You're the best mom." I kissed the top of her head and hugged her closer.

"Aww," she looked up at me with more tears in her eyes, "you're the best dad. I always knew you would be."

"Alright, we're here. We'll clean up the kitchen." Jax winked at me and then smiled softly at Prue. "Violet's in good hands. If you need anything else, call or text us. We're on call."

"Thank you, Jax. I don't know what we'd do without you guys." Prue teared up even more.

"That's what friends are for. We'll expect the same when we have a baby."

"Oh?" Prue asked curiously.

"Someday, hopefully soon," Gabi interjected. "Do you need anything else before you go?"

"No, we have the car seat installed and Holden got my bag. Pray for a fast, but *with* drugs, delivery."

"We'll do that." Gabi hugged Prue and then me. "Get out of here before you end up having the baby at home.

"On it." I wrapped my arm around Prue and helped her out to the car.

Luckily, the hospital wasn't too far from us. I wasn't sure if Prue would have stayed in her seat if it had taken any longer. With each contraction getting worse, she squeezed my hand to the point I was afraid I'd wreck her SUV. Once the hospital came into sight, her grip immediately loosened.

"Holden," she stopped me as she stepped out of the vehicle with a hand to my arm, "I love you, and I'm sorry if I'm a tyrant for the next twenty-four hours."

"I love you too." I leaned down and kissed her until I felt her relax in my arms. "What do you say we get this show on the road?"

"I'd say I already want to smack you. It's not a show. If I could, it would only take a minute, then bam, the baby's born."

"Sorry." I kissed her lips again softly. "Let's get you inside. Maybe they'll put you in next to Alex."

"Oh my god, I can't believe we might have our babies on the same day. Gabi better hurry up and get pregnant so we can all have kids around the same age."

"I'll be sure to let her know," I shook my head as I helped her walk into the hospital.

Twelve very long hours later, our son, Milo, was born, and as Prue rested, exhausted from the long process, I snuck out of the room to call Jax and see how Violet was doing.

"Hey man, got good news?" Jax answered.

"The best. Milo was born at six-forty-two weighing in at seven pounds two ounces and twenty-three inches long."

Jax whistled and relayed the information to Gabi.

"How's Vi doing?" She'd been fine all the other times I'd called, but I knew she was anxious to see her brother.

"She's good. We've been wearing her out."

"Do you think you could keep her for the night? It's too late for her to visit, and I'd like to stay here with Prue."

"No problem. I'll tell her we'll go visit first thing in the morning."

I couldn't help but laugh. "Don't tell her that, or she'll be waking you up at three in the morning asking you to take her."

"Thanks for the heads up. Congrats man."

"Thanks, man. For everything. I should get back in there. Call me if you need me to come home."

"We've got it all under control. We'll see you tomorrow."

Heading back to Prue's room, I spotted Luke outside Alex's room. He was putting his phone in his pocket when I reached him. He looked as exhausted as Prue with dark circles under his eyes, and his hair looked as if he'd run his hand through it a few hundred times. He was a mellow dude, but when the love of your life was in pain and screaming, it could get to the best of any of us.

"You doing okay?" I asked, patting him on the back.

"Yeah, just tired. With Alex being a week overdue, she hasn't been sleeping much and neither have I. How about you?"

"I got more sleep than you, but yeah, it's exhausting. It's worth it though. The baby okay? I know Alex has been worried."

"Everyone's okay. Alex had a miscarriage years ago,

and Mason tried to come early, so she's high risk. Maybe after this one, she won't be." He shrugged.

"Do you think you'll have more?" I was pretty sure Prue was done after all the threats she'd made during the delivery.

"If I can convince her." He grinned. "I say we get some rest, but you know the deal."

"Yeah, sleep when you can. It's going to be rough for a while, and if you were any other man, I'd tell you to help Alex out, but I know you'll do more than your fair share."

"Thanks, man." He slapped me on the back. "That means a lot coming from you. I'll be next door if you need anything."

"Same goes for you. It's pretty awesome our kids were born on the same day."

"Totally fucking awesome," he said a little too loudly for the hospital halls. We were both cracking up as we separated and walked into our respective rooms.

"Hey," Prue greeted me, holding her hand out to me.

I went to her. I always went to her. She was my orbit, and nothing could keep me away. "Fuck, Prue, I'm sorry if I woke you."

"Don't worry, you didn't. Come get into bed with me." She patted the bed with a tiny amount of space available, but I'd make it work.

Wrapping my arms around her, Prue rested her head on my chest. One hand, like always, tracing the tattoos on my arms.

"I'm real proud of you, baby." I kissed the top of her head. "Thank you for giving me a family. Not only our children, who are the most beautiful kids in the world by the way, but also our friends."

She yawned and closed her eyes. Her arm slipped down to my waist to hold me close as she did every night. "We're blessed."

That we were.

The first time I rode into Fairlane, I couldn't see why Prue had moved here, but now I wouldn't go anywhere else. We had the best friends anyone could ask for. Our Fairlane gang had truly become a family to us.

The End

Did you enjoy Unsteady in Love? If so, please consider leaving a review on Goodreads, Amazon, or BookBub. Reviews mean the world to authors especially to authors who are starting out. You can help get your favorite books into the hands of new readers.

I'd appreciate your help in spreading the word and it will only take a moment to leave a quick review. It can be as short or as long as you like. Your review could be the deciding factor or whether or not someone else buys my book.

Want more of Holden and Prue? Sign-up today to get an exclusive bonus scene.

To stay up to date on all my releases subscribe to my newsletter. Each month I give away an Amazon gift card to one lucky subscriber. http://bit.ly/2M3Ci29

ACKNOWLEDGMENTS

My family- your support means so much. Thank you for all of your encouragement and giving me the time to do what makes me happy.

To all my **Romance Rookie girls**. I love each and every one of you. Thank you for being there for me during all my highs as well as my lows.

To all my **author friends**, you know who you are. Thank you for accepting me and making me feel welcome in this amazing community.

To each and every **reader**, **reviewer**, and **blog** - I would be nowhere without you. Thank you for taking a chance on an unknown author.

To **Give Me Books**, you're awesome! I'm so thankful for how easy you make releasing a book.

ABOUT HARLOW

Harlow Layne is an emerging contemporary romance author.

Harlow wrote fanfiction for years before she decided to write Luke and Alex's story that had been swimming in her head for years.

When Harlow's not writing you'll find her online shopping on Amazon, Facebook, or Instagram or hanging out with her family and two dogs.

ALSO BY HARLOW LAYNE

Made in United States
Orlando, FL
15 June 2023

34164060R00154